NAILAH & SAGE

A Love So Strong

TOY

Text **LEOSULLIVAN** to **22828** to join our mailing list! To submit a manuscript for our review, email us at submissions@leolsullivan.com

© 2017
Published by Leo Sullivan Presents
www.leolsullivan.com

❀ Created with Vellum

Chapter One

1-NAILAH

"*A*ww, shit."

I moaned as I tried to enjoy the lovemaking session that me and my boyfriend were partaking in. Only thing is, I wasn't in the mood to be made love to. I wanted, no fuck that, I needed to be fucked in the worst way. I had some pent-up frustration in me, and my anxiety was at an all-time high due to the meeting my boyfriend would attend later. I needed one of those toe-curling, put me to sleep because everything is right with the world orgasms, not just a nut.

I lay flat on my back and spread my legs as wide as I could get them while holding the heels of my feet to make sure he could get deep in my pussy.

"Fuck me, bae, I want you to beat this pussy up. Go harder."

"Nailah, I just want to love you. This pussy so good, I don't want to hurt it. Daaaaamn, bae, I'm about to cum. Just cum with me."

I clenched my pussy walls tight to speed this lovemaking session up and faked the orgasm that I had been longing for. Yeah, my pussy was wet, and it involuntarily came, but that was pussy for you. You could get a massage or a good foot rub, and your pussy could be dripping wet, but there is nothing like the orgasm that you feel building at the tip of your toes moving up through your body.

"Bae, I wish I could lay up in this pussy all day, but I got moves to make," Lox told me as he rolled off of me after he was able to get himself together.

I continued to lay in the bed as he got up and jumped in the shower.

Me and Lox had been together for the past five years. Lox was a caring and gentleman, standing at six feet tall with the perfect caramel complexion. No blemishes, bumps, or scars. Hell, he didn't even have any tattoos. I can still remember him telling me that the body was a temple and it was a sin to mark it. It was funny how he wanted to abide by that sin but disregarded the sin of shacking up and jumping up and down in my pussy when we weren't even married.

Lox catered to my every need except for being that Alpha Male that I craved. When we first met, he treated me like I was a fragile piece of crystal. I thought that once he knew he had me locked down that he would eventually show me his true colors, but the shit never happened. He is the same man today that he was when I met him.

"Nailah, you don't hear me talking to you? You just lying there staring at the ceiling?" Lox said to me, slightly raising his voice.

I was so caught up in my own thoughts that I didn't even realize Lox had gotten out the shower and was already starting to get dressed.

"Damn, bae, my bad. What did you say?"

"I was thinking if things go right with these niggas, Sage and Markos, at the meeting, we could go out and celebrate. A nigga ready to get up out the game," he told me.

"What you mean ready to get out the game? Just because we opened up one business, you think that shit is enough to afford my damn lifestyle? You really need to start thinking before you speak. I'm a kept bitch, and struggle is not in my vocabulary."

"Come on now, Nailah, we don't even know if these niggas official to just be handing money over to them like that. We do this first deal and see how it go, and then we will look into more investments."

"Official? That can't be coming out your mouth right now when you standing there getting dressed like you're about to go to the club on First Friday, with a fucking snapback on at that, instead of an OFFICIAL business meeting. You need to be worried if they going to even take your ass serious."

"What you mean, bae? I'm dressed in Tru's from my head to my feet," he said, looking down at himself like he was fresh to death.

"Whoopty damn do, you dressed in Tru. Big fucking deal. The boosters steal that shit on the regular. The hoes on Section 8 dress in Tru's including their fucking children, especially when you can buy it out the trunk of a bitch car. Step your fucking game up. If you want to be the fucking boss, present yourself as the boss. I know these dudes are official because my dad only deals with the real, and he got more than enough money that I don't even have to deal with this petty shit with you."

"Why the fuck you always gotta bring your daddy up in our shit? While you telling me to boss up, you need to grow the fuck up and be your own fucking woman, and stop riding your daddy dick."

I busted out laughing at his soft ass. If he had put some bass in his voice when he called himself checking me, I probably would have got turned on, but the only thing he did was give me my laugh for the day. I shook my head as Lox went back in the closet, hopefully, to find some different damn gear to put on. He was not about to embarrass me or my father at this meeting tonight.

I heard him mumbling some shit while he was in there changing his clothes. I started not to pay him any attention until I heard him say, "Fuck your bitch ass daddy and everything he stands for. Sick of hearing about his old ass, I'll be glad when the devil opens the doors for him."

Everybody knew I didn't play when it came to my daddy. I admired and respected my daddy to the fullest. My daddy, Geronimo Kahn, was the epitome of an alpha male. He didn't take shit from nobody, not even me. I had any and everything I could have ever wanted courtesy of my father when I was growing up, but it just wasn't given to me. I had to earn it or work for it. My father always told me, 'you may be my only child and a daughter at that, but I'm not raising no damn punk.' So, if Lox thought he was about to disrespect my daddy, he was about to be in for a rude awakening by the time I dealt with him.

I jumped out my bed in all my naked glory and looked at my dresser to pick up something that I could use to knock some sense into Lox's head. I noticed my Kindle, and it had one of those hard protective covers on it, so I wasn't worried about breaking it. I walked my ass in that closet and slapped his ass upside the head with it as hard as I could.

"I don't know if that nut you busted earlier got you feeling yourself, but when it comes to my daddy, you better recognize what lane you supposed to be in. That sideways talking you were just running under your breath makes me feel like you in the wrong lane approaching oncoming traffic the wrong way."

"What the hell, Nailah? Damn, let a nigga apologize. Nailah, I was wrong to bring your daddy in this. It just seems like I'm not good enough for you or I can't live up to your standards of what you think I should be," he tried to fuss.

I didn't even say anything else to him. I just walked right past him into the bathroom to start showering and hopefully wash away some of this tension. I heard the door close as I was drying off. I hoped this nigga didn't embarrass everything that my father had built. He was only the face of what I was truly in control of and nothing more. I had hoped that at some point in time he would catch on and be able to call at least one fucking shot on his own, but as we all can see, I'm still waiting on that.

I wondered why I kept him around a lot more frequently now. My father had no respect for him and only tolerated him because he was with me. Many times over the last five years, my father had told me to get rid of him. I was too busy holding on to the hope that one day he would blossom into the boss that I needed him to be. My father passed the family business to me because I was his only child. I never wanted to be in the family business, but I couldn't tell my father no. Instead, I let Lox be the face of everything.

Judging by how I had to re-dress him, I knew deep down that he would most likely go to this meeting and mess things up. Being that the meeting was set up for them to meet Lox, and not me, I couldn't change things up at the last minute. That would show that we were unprofessional, unorganized, and fucking amateurs. My father's name still carried a tremendous amount of weight, and that's how we got the meeting in the first place. Everyone knew that the Youngs didn't play when it came to doing business. They only dealt with people who were 'worthy' of their time. That's why I didn't understand why Lox was acting like this was just some ordinary meeting.

I hope he doesn't fuck this up for me. I was already running out of reasons to convince my father not to kill him.

2 - LOX

I had to get out of the house with Nailah. I had love for her, but I didn't love her like I did in the beginning. She was a beautiful woman anybody could see that. Once you look at her flawless brown skin, shoulder length, thick, natural hair, and her body—which was fucking amazing—you couldn't deny her beauty. The problem is that lately, her looks have been the only beautiful thing about her. Once she opened her mouth, her bossy ways made her looks non-existent.

Nailah and I have been rocking with each other for years now. She wasn't the type of female you just let walk away without not trying to cuff her. Cuffing her is exactly what I did. I did all of that before I knew her father was the one and only Geronimo Kahn. Geronimo was the one running shit back in the day, and when I say shit, I mean everything illegal shit.

When it was time for him to get out the game, with him only having one kid, he gave Nailah control of everything. The problem came in when she didn't want to be associated with it, so that's when she came to me. I was supposed to be the face of everything now that her dad was out. Things were supposed to be set up to where everyone thought that I was the one running everything. All decisions were discussed with Nailah, though.

At first, I was cool with how everything was set up. Somewhere down the line, I noticed that not only did Nailah start talking to me crazy, but she didn't respect a nigga's thoughts. It was like everything I said or did wasn't good enough for her or her father. Just like now, she got me going to meet with the Youngs.

Now, the Youngs are larger than her father. I think the Young brothers are on the level with El Chapo and Escobar, but they had two of the sons who were somewhat legit. I say somewhat legit because one was an accountant and the other was a lawyer. They used what they did to make sure the paperwork and stuff looked legit. They had shit legit as fuck because it seemed like they were winning like a motherfucker.

I didn't want to involve them in what we had going on because it made it look like we didn't know what we were doing. In my eyes, it made us look weak to go beg them niggas for help. Whenever I told Nailah's ass that, all she said was that I wasn't looking at the bigger picture. Lately, I've been keeping my thoughts to myself because she didn't respect them anyway.

I know I had to get to the meeting, but I needed to stop by DeJa's house first. She always helped me relax and focus on making the moves I needed to make. DeJa is my shawty. Call me what you want, like I give a fuck. Nailah is the reason DeJa's even in the picture. She lets me be the man in the relationship.

I can sex her up the way I want to without her laying there faking and calling out for me to do more in the bed. Did I know that Nailah has been faking her orgasms? Hell yeah, I knew. Women don't understand that the pussy does certain shit when you have an orgasm. They thought that flexing your Kegels and yelling was enough to make a man think they were getting theirs. In the beginning, it had me feeling some type of way that Nailah was always faking hers. After a while, I just said fuck it. If she wanted to fake 'em, that was on her. I was gonna get mine, though, so fuck everything else.

I pulled up to DeJa's spot and hopped out. I didn't have

much time, but I needed her to help me relax. I still had the argument with Nailah on my mind. I was still pissed that she had a nigga change clothes to impress some niggas she didn't even fucking know. I used my key to walk up in DeJa's house like I always did.

"DeJa, where you at?" I called out.

I found her in her bedroom cleaning up. She turned around to look at me and stopped in her tracks when she saw how I was dressed.

"What's up with the suit?"

"I have a meeting with the Youngs today. I'm on my way there now, but I need you to bless me with that mouth of yours so I can relax."

She put up whatever she had in her hand. DeJa wasn't runway gorgeous like Nailah, but she was 'hood' pretty. She had all the hood shit that girls had. The weave down to the top of her ass, fake nails always in bright ass colors, rings on her fingers, a wrist full of bracelets, a nose ring, and her top lip was pierced. Her body was alright; she wasn't a brick house, but she wasn't too skinny either. She was a red chick, though, and always watched ratchet TV. She worked, but only part-time because she didn't want her state benefits to be cut off completely.

"I don't know why you didn't get wifey to suck you off," DeJa's smart ass said.

She always brought Nailah up, but I ignored her just like I did all the other times. I don't see the point of her always bringing Nailah up if she was gonna do what I came for anyway. It just felt wrong for me to be talking about Nailah while she's licking the tip of the dick.

"Less talking and more sucking," I told her.

I felt her mouth encase my dick, and I let my eyes close, mouth drop open, and head fall back.

"Slow down, girl."

She did just as she was told and slowed down on massaging

and sucking my dick. If I could keep her mouth with me all the time, I would. Her fucking head was amazing. I mean, like having you want to go find the nigga who taught her the shit that her mouth did. I didn't have to touch her head or stroke her mouth like it was a pussy. She did all the right shit on her own. All I had to do was relax and let her do what she does.

"Oh fuck, catch that shit, Dee," I called out.

DeJa swallowed all my stress as it shot down her throat. She stood up and opened her mouth to show me that she didn't miss a drop. It made me smile that she was so eager to make a nigga happy. Even if I did just fuck Nailah a little bit ago. She went to the bathroom and brushed her teeth and tongue because she knew not to talk to me with dick and balls breath.

"You need to step up and show all of them that you know what you doing. It don't make no sense that you basically being a fuck boy for your precious Nailah," she said.

"What I tell you about speaking on her? Was I a fuck boy a few minutes ago when the tip of my dick was touching your tonsils? You can't complain about her if you out here being a whole side chick and shit. You don't like that I'm still with her or how she handles me then walk the fuck away. Ain't nobody holding yo ass hostage. Play your position or get the fuck out the rotation."

I know she just heard me say I had a meeting to go to, and I needed some relief, not more stress. Yet, here she was acting like she didn't know her place in my life. We didn't walk into this with me hiding shit.

"One day you gon' realize that I'm the realest one on your team. You gon' miss me when I'm gone. I'm not gonna play the side chick much longer. You need to get your shit together."

I looked at her and couldn't help but laugh.

"Yeah, alright. I NEVER told you that I was gonna leave Nailah. I mean, damn, a few times when you gave me head, I was on the phone with her. So, why would you even think you getting a promotion in my life? Look, I don't need this shit right now. You gonna make me late for this damn meeting talking stupid."

I checked my slacks to make sure she didn't get any cum on my pants, and I fucking left. This morning was not working out in my favor already. Both of my chicks were out of their fucking minds.

3 - SAGE

I looked through the file again as I sat in my office. We were about to meet with this clown ass nigga as a favor to my father and uncles. We already had a dossier on this nigga Lox and Nailah. Nailah was the daughter of the hood legend, Geronimo Kahn. Our families had an extensive history. Geronimo was the nigga who had the potential to be on the same level as my family. He supplied most of the East Coast and Midwest.

When I asked my father why didn't Geronimo try to get on our level, he kicked me the realest answer I've ever heard. He told me straight up that Geronimo knew he couldn't do this shit all of his life and remain a free man. Geronimo didn't have siblings and only had one child, which was his daughter, Nailah. He knew he would pass everything to Nailah, even though she didn't want any parts of it. So, instead of having her handle more than he knew she could or wanted, he got out and passed what he had to her. I had to respect Geronimo because he knew when to walk away. Greed is the main thing that is niggas' downfall in the game these days.

I understood where Nailah was coming from too because I was in a somewhat similar situation. My name is Sage Monte

Young. My family is the infamous Youngs. My entire family had their asses in the streets except me and my cousin Markos. We were the only ones who had opted to go to college. The family was fine with that as long as we went for something that could help the family.

I was a corporate accountant, but I also had my law degree, while Markos was a corporate lawyer. We didn't only work for the family, but whoever we did work with had to be cleared by the family. We did complete background checks on potential clients and their significant others. In addition to the background checks, we worked with a PI firm that followed them around for two months before the meetings were even scheduled. Which brings me back to this bullshit I was reading now.

"You reading that shit again like you don't have it memorized already," Markos said as he walked into my office without knocking.

"Do you ever knock?" I asked.

"For what? Your secretary is old enough to be GG's sister, so I know you not in here knocking her down. You doing what you always do at work, which is work. When you start having lunch fuck sessions, I'll start knocking," he said and laughed.

"Whatever. But, yeah, I'm trying to understand what she sees in this basic ass nigga. From the pictures, she fine as a mother fucker. We got her medical records, so all that beauty is natural, which is rare as fuck. She's smart too, so I'm not understanding why they together," I explained.

"Man calm down. If she wanna be with a clown, let her do that. I talked to my pops, and he wants us to work with them even though dude bogus."

I sat back and thought about what Markos was saying. My dad told me the same thing when I talked to him this morning.

"It's ten minutes 'til, and the nigga not even here yet. Strike one," Markos said.

Markos was a clown, but when it came to business, he was sharp as a mother fucker. We were all about being punctual and professional, which I could tell this Lox cat wasn't, and he hadn't even shown his face yet. Markos and I talked until my secretary called over the intercom that Lox had finally shown up five minutes after we were supposed to start. I told her to send him back.

This nigga walked in dressed in designer labels from head to toe, but he looked out of place and uncomfortable as fuck right now.

"What's up, fam?" Lox said.

Markos shook his head but kept his mouth shut. He didn't hold his hand out to shake either of our hands, so I sat back down to get this over quickly.

"How can we help you?" I asked.

"Alright, so look. I'm opening up this little boutique to help clean up some of our cash and shit. I know y'all can help us make our shit look straight on paper so we won't have to worry about twelve coming to get at us," Lox said.

I was quiet for a minute because I couldn't believe this was the nigga that Geronimo's daughter was dealing with on this level. His posture was off. It looked like he was trying to sit up straight to impress us. He just didn't know we had his ass pegged soon as he walked in. For one, he didn't look either of us in the eye. Secondly, he looked like it was hard for him to walk in the shoes he had on. Which means she dressed his ass for this meeting.

"So, you saying you want us to launder your money and legitimize your standing in the business community without the hassle of getting audited or investigated," Markos said with irritation in his tone.

"Yeah, that's what I said," this fool answered.

Markos adjusted himself in his seat. I knew Markos was about to go off on dude, so I stepped in.

"We have some information on you to review. In the meantime, we would like to invite you to dinner tonight. It will be with a few family members and their significant others. If you care to join us, I will have my secretary call you with the details in an hour or two."

He was sitting there like he didn't understand what I just said.

"We having dinner with a few of our people tonight. You need to be there and bring ya girl. His secretary gonna hit you up with the details in a couple of hours," Markos said.

Markos was at the point where he wanted to punch dude in the face. I found it funny because Markos had absolutely no patience for stupid shit. The way he was sitting there in a designer suit and shoes looking like a lil boy whose mom made him wear a suit to church was comical. The fact that he didn't know how to articulate himself properly was fucking sad.

"Nigga, we good. You can go now," Markos said.

He nodded his head and walked out of the office.

"I'm gonna fuck around and shoot his dumb ass. What the fuck you invite them to dinner for?" Markos said as soon as the door closed.

"I need to see what is making their operation work. Obviously, it's not his dumb ass. They bringing in too much money for him to be like he is. There has to be a reason for it."

"I guess. Let me get out of here so I can find a date that won't make me choke her ass before the end of dinner tonight," Markos said.

Him saying that made me realize I had to let Leslie know we were going to dinner tonight. I really didn't want to take her, but I had no other choice. She was my fiancée who I really was tired of. She was aware that what we once had was long gone, but after being with her for damn near ten years, we were just used to each other. Lately, we'd been going through the motions. I could have easily tried to put the fire back in our relationship, but I felt that if we were supposed to be together, our relationship wouldn't have fizzled out in the first place. I didn't want to talk to her, so I chose to text instead.

Me: *We going to dinner with some associates tonight. Be ready by 8*

Her: *this is late notice I need to get my hair done and buy something to wear*

Me: *all those dresses in the closet that still got tags on it. You don't need to buy nothing*

Her: *that's all outdated stuff. I need something that is in this season or hasn't been released yet*

I shook my head at her because this was part of the problem. When I got with her, she was a chick who wanted something out of life. She was working two jobs to make sure she was good and didn't have to ask anybody for nothing. Somewhere down the line, she ended up being that chick who sat around the fucking house all day waiting for the next party or vacation weekend so she could front for her girls. I needed a chick who was on my fucking level, and she just wasn't doing it like that no more.

———

I say at the table hoping my face wasn't revealing my thoughts. The stinking perfume that Leslie had on helped keep my dick from being totally hard. The pictures that were in her dossier did her no justice. She was fucking beautiful, and that was a damn understatement. Seeing her with him let me know that she was the one calling the shots. I could see that shit as soon as she walked into the room. She hadn't said a fucking word, and she had the attention of everyone in this motherfucker.

"Is she the one you are going to be doing business with?" Leslie asked.

I looked at her to let her know that she needed to pipe down with the attitude. She had been acting all pissed off since Nailah and Lox sat down at the table.

"They are both potential clients," I said to her, hoping that would shut her up.

"I think she's trying too hard if you ask me. I mean, her coming here with the same color you're wearing had to be planned," Leslie said with her face turned up.

"No, it wasn't. I've never met Sage or Markos in person until tonight. So, if we happen to be matching then maybe I'm better suited to be by his side than you," Nailah said with a smirk on her face.

She definitely had a sauciness about herself. She wasn't going to let Leslie talk to her crazy, but she didn't have to come out of character to do it. Definitely boss bitch in the making. She couldn't be a total boss bitch yet because she still had fuck boy on her arm. I had a feeling that was about to change sooner or later.

"He doesn't frequent dance clubs that have poles, so how would you all meet?" Leslie said with a smirk on her face.

"I guess at the same Rainbow store you bought that dress," Nailah said before sipping the wine from her glass.

Markos with his dumb ass fell out laughing. I could only shake my head because I told Leslie's dumb ass that she needed to put something else on. The thing was that she was trying to make me feel some type of way because of what she had on. She wasn't hurting me or my image, so I stopped arguing about it.

I could see that things were gonna get out of hand if these two kept going back and forth.

"You look beautiful tonight, Nailah. You're definitely one of the most beautiful women I have seen tonight," Markos said.

I knew he was throwing shade at Leslie. He never liked her. I did try to hide my smile when he said that and looked at Leslie. I knew we were gonna be arguing in the car, but I just didn't care right now.

I was ignoring Markos because he was too busy laughing at the fact that Lox and I had on the same black Tom Ford suit with red pinstripes, red Tom Ford shirt, with a black and red tie. The difference came in with Nailah wearing a red Gucci dress with some Givenchy pumps decorated with diamonds. Leslie was by my side, but she was upset because of what I said about her shopping, so her petty ass was wearing a basic ass black dress.

For her to be so concerned about how people saw her, she was losing tonight like a mother fucker.

I could tell Nailah was pissed at how Lox was acting, but she never let that show in her demeanor. She still was about her business. I picked up on the little things like how she was the one answering most of the questions. Even when I complimented her on her color choice, she responded by telling me that red was the color that represented power and control. I already knew that though because that was the reason I wore it.

"You know y'all have on the same suit," Markos said laughing.

"Oh yeah, I didn't even notice. That's some wild shit, huh?" this dumb nigga said.

I shook my head because he was nowhere near being worthy of sitting at this table with us. Shit, to be honest, he didn't deserve to be with her period. I think Markos picked up on it because he was firing off question after question, and this nigga, Lox, was not answering shit.

"You know what? Fuck this," I said standing up.

Markos stood up after me because he knew what time it was.

"This dinner is over. I can't take no more of this bullshit," I said.

Markos pulled out the chair for his date and Leslie because I was leaning over the table. Lox looked like he thought he was going to die while Nailah sat there stone-faced waiting for me to finish talking.

"When we agreed to meet with you all, we agreed to meet with the BOSS, not the middleman. If you want this business relationship to begin then the middle man needs to be cut out of the equation. When we sit at a table, we only sit with BOSSES nothing less. So, let me know when the BOSS is ready to show HER face. Until then, we have nothing else to discuss," I told her.

I gave Markos the head nod because I was damn sure leaving. I didn't have time for this bullshit. I wasn't into playing games.

"Says the nigga who is designer down, but his bitch is

wearing a basic ass clearance rack dress. You want to sit at tables with bosses but run your dick up in a basic ass bitch. That makes a lot of sense," Nailah said and rolled her eyes.

"Don't worry about where my eleven inches go. You couldn't handle my shit, so why you worried about it? We only dealing with y'all on the strength of ya pops. You and your mouth are gonna make me forget all about that shit and say fuck it," I told her.

I heard Leslie kissing her teeth behind me.

"Oh, you can talk shit about my man, but I can't come for Tasha? Sensitive aren't you, for a boss nigga," Nailah said with a smirk.

"Her name isn't Tasha."

"Oh, it's not? I thought her name was as basic as the dress she has on," Nailah said.

"Call me when you ready to deal with the big boys and surround yourself with bosses instead of fuck boys."

I dropped my napkin on the table. After leaving the money for the bill along with a sizeable tip. I shook my head because Lox didn't even offer to pay the bill, but we were supposed to believe that he was a boss. I gave her my card and left. The ball was in her court now; she could either step out in the open or find somebody else to work with. I knew she would be calling because we were the best at what we did, so now all I had to do was wait.

Chapter Four

3 - NAILAH

"How that nigga know I'm not the one calling the shots?" Lox barked as soon as we got in the car.

I knew he really didn't want me to answer him. Shit, if he wanted to know he should have asked Sage himself before he walked away from the table. I'm sure he wouldn't hesitate to tell him.

"If you gonna have me out here as the face of this shit, you need to let me be a man and do man shit. You answering all they fucking questions. How you expect them to respect me if you keep opening your fucking mouth?"

"Did you know the answers?" I asked sarcastically.

I knew he didn't know about the shit they were asking, which is why I answered. Lox was too worried about the wrong shit right now. Instead of wondering how he could step his game up, he wanted me to be the quiet piece of arm candy. Hell, I wanted to be that, but the only way that was going to happen was if I was on someone else's arm. I needed a man who knew how to wear a suit and not let the suit wear him. A man who you could tell was a boss just by looking at him. Sage would be my ideal nigga if he wasn't engaged already. I wasn't into breaking up homes or being a side chick, so my search continues.

"What the hell, Nailah? I'm talking to you, and you not fucking listening, just like this morning. What the fuck is going on with your ass?"

"Nothing. I'm thinking about our next move. I'm gonna have to go talk to my father in the morning. I know he will help me figure this out," I told him.

I knew that he was gonna go off because I said my father's name, but what the fuck did he think I was going to say?

"I'm so fucking tired of hearing about your damn daddy. He don't run shit no more, WE do. You need to realize that shit. I'm sick of this shit. You gonna fuck around and make me do some shit that I don't want to do. Keep playing with my ass," Lox fussed.

If I cared about what he was saying, I might have debated with him on some of the shit he just said. The thing was that I didn't care; he didn't run a damn thing but his mouth. If he wasn't fucking with me, he probably wouldn't be more than a corner boy. I finally realized that tonight. He didn't once try to answer a question or try to stand up for himself. Little did he know, his ass was on the way out the door. I was getting too damn old to keep wasting my time with him.

"I'm gonna go check on a few things after I drop you off. Don't wait up," he said.

I looked at him like he was crazy. I started to say something, but then I decided not to. There wasn't a need, honestly. Whoever the bitch was that he was fucking with could have him and his lame ass strokes.

He pulled up to the house, and I got out the car. Simple as that was, and as loud as any other grown man would have had something to say because of the disrespectful manner in which I got out of the car, Lox said absolutely nothing. I ran some bath water then got in the bed to look at something on TV. My phone rang, and it was my father. I wasn't expecting him to call tonight, but since he did, I might as well get this over with.

"Hello," I answered.

"My driver is outside. Put some clothes on, get in the car, and leave that nothing ass nigga of yours where he is."

The call ended before I could reply. I wasn't about to tell him that Lox wasn't there. The sound of his voice let me know that he knew how bad the dinner was. I threw on a jogging suit and some slides and headed out to the car to get my tongue lashing from my father. I was expecting to get in the car and have a few minutes to have a drink or two before I had to face him. He had other plans because he was in the back seat when I got in there.

"Hi, Daddy," I said, trying to sound innocent.

"Cut the bullshit, Nailah Renae. I told you when you got with that mother fucker that he wasn't the one for you. I keep telling you this over and over, but you don't want to face the facts. He's not on your level, and he never will be. Some people just are not supposed to be bosses. I understand you don't want to be in the forefront, but he has to go. Now, how he goes is up to you. He can go walking on his own two or being carried by six," my father told me.

I looked at my daddy, and I knew that he was livid at what went on tonight. His light brown skin had a red tint to it like it always did when he was pissed. My daddy was still handsome to be in his early sixties. He stood six feet even, and he still was in the gym four days a week, so he had defined muscles. His beard had grey in it, but it made him look more distinguished than it made him look old.

"Daddy, I understand what you're saying. I know he needs to go now. He showed me that tonight," I said honestly.

"You're going to have to deal with the Youngs on your own. I don't want any fuck ups on this. This is a major move for you. That piece of shit will bring the Kahn family name down, and I will kill him myself before I allow that to happen. I'll give you some time to get things together, but not much. You need to figure this out and fix this shit," he told me in a harsh tone.

My father leaned over and gave me a kiss on the cheek. That was his subtle way of dismissing me. I got out of the car and hoped I could convince Sage to deal with me and me only. I knew he was most likely with his chick tonight, but seeing how pissed my father was, I had no reason to wait for the morning to come. I plopped down on my bed and dialed the number on the card he gave me. The phone only rang once before he answered.

"This is Sage."

"Sage, this is Nailah. I would like to have a meeting with you and Markos as soon as possible."

"Just you, right?" he asked.

"Yes, just me," I answered.

"Markos is busy right now, but I can meet you in twenty minutes at the twenty-four-hour Starbucks on Fletcher street."

I sat up on the bed because I was not expecting him to want to meet with me tonight.

"Tonight?" I asked.

"Either you want to get this shit moving or not. You telling me you let your lame ass nigga put you on a curfew? I thought you was the boss. If you the boss, get your ass up and meet me in twenty minutes." He chuckled.

He ended the call before I could disagree or agree. I got up and slid my feet in my slides, thankful that I hadn't taken my clothes off yet. I grabbed my keys and headed out the door.

When I got to the Starbucks, he was already there waiting for me in his car. I knew that this was only one of his many cars, but the car fit him very well. It was a 1971 Plymouth Hemi Cuda in midnight blue, which I thought was black until I got closer to the car. I was almost to the door of the coffee shop, but he called out to me and stopped me from going in.

"Nailah, hop in," he said after rolling the window down.

"I thought we were going to talk here."

"We not. Get in the car with me and leave your ride here. That nigga probably got a tracking device on your shit," he said with a smile.

"You not gonna keep making comments about..." I started to fuss as I got in.

The sight of him in the driver's seat wearing some grey basketball shorts with a wife beater distracted me from finishing what I was going to say. He was dressed down, but he smelled like he was going to work or something. I don't know what kind of games he was playing, but this shit had me on edge and my panties wet.

"Say what you was 'bout to say. What's on your mind?"

"Why are we riding around in your car? Nice choice, by the way. You don't see too many 1971 Cudas around anymore. People usually go for the '69 Charger or the '68 Shelby."

"Well, I don't worry about what everybody else goes for. How you know about cars?" he asked with a questioning look on his face.

"I'm my dad's only child, so I guess you could say I was his son and daughter wrapped up in one. I went to etiquette and dance classes during the week and to the gun range and races on the weekend," I told him convincingly.

That wasn't really what I wanted to know, but I couldn't let what I was thinking float out of my mouth either.

"Well, we in my car because I know there are no bugs or none of that bullshit in here. It's bulletproof, so we both are protected. Also, as you can see, I'm not exactly dressed to be seen out in public right now."

I looked down at his basketball shorts again like I didn't notice them when I first got in the car.

"We could have waited until tomorrow or the next day to get this done."

"We could've, but why? We were both up and not doing a damn thing, so why not get business done when the opportunity presents itself? If you couldn't make it, you would have said so. I will let you know now that I don't have office hours. When something needs to be addressed, I do the shit. No need for waiting. The next hour among the living is not guaranteed, so do what you can when you can."

He continued to drive, but I wasn't paying attention to where we were going. I was relaxed and content.

"What type of boutique you have?" he asked.

"Does it matter?"

"Not really, but the fact that you are such a borderline bitch does. We're here to help each other, so all the smart-ass shit that flies out of your mouth needs to stop. I can't work with people if I'm thinking of ways to make them scream," he said.

My head turned to him so quick I had to laugh at myself.

"From choking you, of course," he added with a smirk.

"It's a plus sized boutique. Catering to women who are a size twelve and up."

"Why did you choose that demographic? You're not plus sized from what I can tell," he said.

"When I was in school, I was friends with this girl. She was a size eighteen in high school. She got bullied, joked on, harassed, and embarrassed daily. One day she just stopped coming to school. Then, one day out of nowhere we had an assembly, and that's when we found out that she had killed herself because of the severe depression she suffered. I went to her house, and her mother gave me a note she left for me. I was the only friend she had in the whole fucking school.

"Her letter told me how she just wanted to feel beautiful on the outside. She felt that if the outside was beautiful, then people would want to know the inside of her. So, when my father came to me and said that I needed to open a legit business that wasn't a club, soul food restaurant, cleaners, or car wash, that was the first thing that came to mind. The boutique isn't high priced at all. There is no piece in there priced over $250.00. Yeah, I take a hit on the more expensive pieces, but it's worth it if it stops some woman from doing what my friend did."

I didn't notice that he had pulled over while I was talking. He looked like he wasn't expecting me to say what I had just told him. The crazy part was that he was the first one who had ever asked why I wanted a plus-sized boutique. Lox never cared to even ask me that question.

5 - SAGE

I went to my pops house after work today. I needed to talk to him about this whole situation with Kahn and bounce some ideas off him. I had been going over Nailah's portfolio for the last two days. Even though the little boutique she had was a good look, it wasn't enough. They were bringing in way too much money for them to expect a boutique to make them look legit. I know she mentioned that her dad didn't want to invest in the 'typical black businesses,' so I would have to present other options to her.

I looked down at my phone, which was ringing again with Leslie on the other end. She'd been blowing me up since I dropped her ass off after dinner that night. I ignored her ass as I stepped into the house that I grew up in.

"Your ass finally decided to show up, huh, lil nigga?" my pops said.

"You know I'm a busy man. I'm here now, that's all that matters, right?"

He looked at me with his signature 'stop trying to bullshit me' look. As he smoked his cigar, he held out his hand to tell me to sit down. My pops was an OG to the fullest. He didn't say much, but when he did, you damn sure better listen. Even at the age of sixty-three, he could easily pass for my older brother. Yes, he used that shit to his advantage when it came to the women.

My mom had passed away over ten years ago, and that was the only time I saw my father cry. He didn't have a girlfriend or even a lady that he kept around on the regular. He still wore his wedding ring all these years later.

I wanted that kind of love one day. She had been dead and gone for a long ass time, but he was still loyal to her. Yeah, he did hit up the strip club champagne rooms, but he would always say that once you give your heart, ain't no getting it back. He still went to her grave once a month like clockwork and sat there for hours.

"What's the deal with the Kahn situation?" he asked.

"They're making too much money to have anybody believe that boutique is bringing that kind of money in. I'm gonna have a meeting with the daughter next week to discuss some more options. They need to invest in at least six more business to make the shit look legit on paper," I explained.

"Do you think she would fight you on your suggestions? I hear she is something of a difficult thang to deal with."

"She'll listen to me," I told him.

I guess I said that with too much confidence. Pops looked up at me then sat back in his chair.

"You still with that Lisa chick?"

"Leslie, her name is Leslie," I told him.

"You still with her or not?"

"Yeah, we still together."

"You don't sound happy about it. Is she showing her true colors yet?" he asked.

Pops always said that Leslie had an agenda when it came to our relationship. He met her one time and told me in front of her that she wouldn't last long. I never asked why he felt that way, but I also kept her at arm's length. She had a few items at my place but never too much, and she rarely stayed the night.

There was no exchange of keys, pop ups, or none of that other shit.

"She acted out a little bit the other night at dinner with Nailah and Lox. A few of the family was there, but she was more pissed about Nailah than anything else," I told him.

"Your cousin told me all about it. My question is, did you set her straight in the car?"

"Of course. I know the drill. You can't chastise your woman in front of others. That is only to be done in the comfort of your own home. Always do it face to face, and never around others," I told him.

Pops nodded his head. He had that far off look in his eyes. I knew he was thinking about my mother because that was the look he would get.

"I'm glad you paid attention to something. So, when are you gonna dismiss Luann?" he asked.

"Leslie, Pops, her name is Leslie," I told him again.

"You know who I'm talking about. It doesn't matter because her ass is irrelevant anyway. You need to end things with her. I told you a long time ago that she's not the one. I don't know why you are wasting your time anyway. Tell me about little Nailah. What was she doing that had Lu Lu's panties in a bunch at dinner?" he asked.

I didn't bother to correct him this time. I knew he was doing the shit on purpose, so I just shook my head.

"Pops, she wasn't doing nothing but being her. Leslie got pissed when she saw that Nailah's dress matched my suit to the tee. I mean, you would have thought we were a couple if we stood beside each other. Markos with his bullshit didn't help when Leslie called herself throwing shade. Nailah wasn't having that shit, though. She came right back at Leslie. Shit, she even came for me after I threw some shots at that nigga Lox," I told him.

"She was always a feisty one. I remember Ronimo having to

go up to the school because she done said or done something to somebody."

Pops laughed at the memories. I was confused because I didn't remember meeting her before the dinner.

"You knew her when she was little? I know you and Geronimo were close, but I don't remember her," I said as I tried to understand what was going on.

Pops got up and walked into his office. I didn't go anywhere because I figured he was coming back. When he did come back, he had the box with all the old pics in it from when we were young as fuck. He dropped the box in front of me and gave me a head nod.

I opened the box and started pulling out pictures of all of us kids playing and other stuff around the house.

"Pops, who's this little girl?" I asked.

I hated when he played Blue's Clues with me. He always did this shit because he wanted you to figure it out on your own.

"You don't remember the little girl that used to come over here, and you and your cousins would beat her up until she started fighting y'all bad asses back? Markos and Montay used to call her Doll Baby because your mom would call her a precious doll baby."

"I remember she bit Montay 'til he bled." I laughed at the memory.

We used to torture her back then. She used to come over a lot, but when I turned eight, she stopped coming around.

"Where is she now? We used to treat her like she was our little sister. She hated that shit."

"Well, you saw her the other day. Y'all were looking like a couple from what you just told me," he said with a big ass smile on her face.

"Nailah is Doll Baby?"

"It damn sure ain't Lula May, but she's the one you call your girlfriend. So, let me ask you this. The other night, did you get that little sister vibe from Nailah, or was it something else?" Pops asked and laughed.

I had to laugh because he knew damn well I wasn't looking at her like a sister.

"Lu-Lu may be a little shady, but she damn sure is not crazy. She was fucking with Nailah because she knows what y'all are too stubborn and blind to see. Get your ass out. I gotta go hit up a titty bar in a few," he said as he stood up.

"Pops, you need to stay away from those damn strip clubs."

"You need to keep your ass away from Liza. Now we both know something that the other needs to handle. Get out, nigga," Pops said.

I shook my head and left like he told me to. I was too busy trying to avoid the fact that Nailah was Doll Baby. The question was, what were our fathers up to? Why didn't they tell us all of that before now?

Chapter Six

6 - NAILAH

"What's the deal with them Youngs?"

Lox had been asking me about what was going on with the Youngs since the dinner that night. He had been staying out later and later lately. I knew what the deal was, but right now I was too focused on making this shit work with the Youngs to be concerned about what bitch he was fucking.

"I'm taking care of it," I told him.

"What the fuck is that supposed to mean? If I'm supposed to be the face of this shit, I need to know what's going on, Nailah. What the fuck is the big deal? Since when we got secrets?"

I didn't want to tell him how I really felt, at least not right now. If he kept pushing, he was gonna get something he wasn't expecting.

"Are the drops going okay? Is the shipment still on time for next week?" I asked.

He looked at me like I was out of line for asking him those questions.

"Everything's good," he said.

Lox was gonna keep fucking with me, and he was gonna come up missing. I hated when he started acting like a little bitch. He just didn't know, but he was showing me more and

more every day that I should have just ran everything like my
father wanted me to. I rolled my eyes and walked out of the
room. If I kept talking to him, we would be arguing, then he
would leave like he's been doing lately.

"So, you not gonna ask me for details?" he asked.

"Why would I do that? It's obvious that you don't want to
tell me the details. I'm not gonna beg you for them. If I really
wanted to find out, I could, and you would never know the
difference. I think me letting you be the face of this is getting to
your head. This is still my shit," I told him.

"There it is, the famous line you've been saying a lot. This is
your shit. We all know that, but out on the street, I'm the one
everybody comes to. You just keep playing your role. You all
hush-hush about what the fuck is going on with them Youngs.
Don't let me find out you out here fucking them niggas. I'm
telling you now if I find out it's some shit going on, I don't give a
fuck who your fucking daddy is, I'm beating both y'all asses," he
said, trying to put some fear in me.

I heard him loud and clear, but now it was time for him to
hear my ass. I was all for the man being the man, but him threatening me over some shit that's not happening was about all I
could take for the day. I knew my flat irons were still plugged up
from when I did my hair earlier. I went in the bathroom,
unplugged the flatirons, and tossed them in the air. Just like I
thought, his dumb ass caught them with his bare hands.

Lox screamed out in pain as he dropped them and grabbed
his hand.

"I'm gonna fuck you up for this shit," he yelled.

"The next time you threaten me, it won't be a flat iron that
you'll be catching, mother fucker. Be happy your hand is the only
thing burned."

This motherfucker was pressing his fucking luck. If my father
found out that he was in there threatening me and shit, he
wouldn't last to see tomorrow. I walked past him, leaving him
standing there holding his burned hand. I heard his phone ring-

ing, but I paid it no mind because I had to meet Sage and Markos. The way he just talked to me let me know that he was on some creep shit. It was just a matter of time before he got caught.

I got myself together and headed out just in time for the meeting with Youngs. I hoped they had some good news because I needed something to take my mind off Lox right now. When I got to their office building, there was another guy in Sage's office. I had never seen him before, but the way they were laughing and joking, I figured he was either a close friend or a cousin.

When I stepped into the office, they all stopped and looked at me like I was a fucking art exhibit or something. Men gawk at me every day, but this was something totally different. I was fighting the urge to turn around and walk out because I was so uncomfortable.

"Hello, umm is there a need for me to come back?" I asked.

They all stood there looking crazy.

"Nah, come on in. Have a seat. This is our cousin, Montay. He just stopped by to talk shit and lose a bet," Markos said.

I reached out to shake his hand, but this nigga hugged me like I was a long-lost relative. I stepped out of his embrace, and this nigga acted like he didn't want to let me go.

"Tay, back the hell up, nigga," Sage barked.

"Oh shit. You right. My bad, baby girl, you just look like somebody we used to know. I'm not on no creep shit or nothing like that, but this shit is crazy as fuck."

Montay favored Sage and Markos, but he was dark skinned with a beard. He looked like he could be a male IG model. I bet he had all kinds of tattoos all over his body. His hair showed that he had some Caribbean or Indian in his family.

"If you staying, nigga, sit down. If not, get the fuck out. Stop fucking staring at her. Damn," Sage said.

I sat down, ready to get business done and get the hell out of there.

"How ya nigga feel about us wanting to deal with you and not him?" Markos asked.

"It doesn't really matter how he feels. He's gonna have to deal with it either way."

"True, but I would hate to have to fuck him up because he's feeling some type of way," Markos said.

I got a funny vibe from Markos when he said that. His tone sounded protective, but it didn't make sense for him to try to protect me. We were just doing business together.

"That nigga ain't stupid," Montay said.

"Okay, what the hell is going on here? Why is everyone so concerned about my well-being all of a sudden? Trust me, fellas, I'm not concerned about him or any other nigga coming at me stupid. Can we get down to business now?" I asked.

They all looked at each other and started laughing.

"Chill, man. We just don't want to have you out here getting hurt behind some insecure ass ride along nigga," Sage said.

"Okay, so what is the deal with my portfolio?"

I wanted to get the meeting underway so I could be on my way.

"I looked at the profile, and you need to open or invest in at least five more businesses for everything to look right on paper. I recommend that you pick up a few franchises and maybe even a high-class spa. This way, you will have enough business to compensate your extra income. When and if the IRS comes looking, they will only find what they need to find."

"How can you be so sure that they won't find anything else?" I asked.

"Trust me, I got you. Ain't shit gonna go down while I'm working on your shit."

The way he looked at me gave me a chill and made me nervous. There was a tone of finality in what he said and coupled with his look, I knew he wasn't playing around.

"Is there something I need to know? There is a weird vibe in here. If you don't want to work with me, just let me know. I'm a big girl, I can handle it."

They all just looked at each other with smirks on their faces.

"Nah, we definitely gonna work with ya. Don't worry, you will be set for life by this time next year. I'm talking on paper and off paper. As long as you trust us and keep fuck boy number one out of our shit, we will always be good."

I nodded my head slowly because I was still a little skeptical about them being upfront with me. Something was definitely up, but I couldn't put my finger on what it was exactly.

"I can transfer the investment funds that you need in the morning. I know that it will be some insane amount, so they most likely will be available within ten business days. I know you need the investment funds to be traceable, so that is why I need to use a bank, correct?" I asked.

"You got it. I will text you the amount before the night is over. I just ask that you make sure to keep your nigga out of our shit. If he comes snooping around, he will be handled," Sage told me.

I sat there wondering how they expected me to respond to what they said. I could have been the concerned girlfriend, but that would be fake as fuck right now. Most likely, Lox was cheating on me with at least one multi-colored weave wearing hood rat. I was not going to play like shit was cool on the home front. These niggas would probably see through that shit anyway. So, instead of playing myself and acting some kind of way, I just nodded my head and walked out. If Lox went against what I told him as far as him staying out of what I had going on with the Youngs, then he was gonna have to deal with the consequences.

After leaving out of the office building and getting in my car, I called my dad to give him the update on what I had just found out. He would be happy that I was indeed working with them and that Lox was out of the loop. He had never liked Lox, but lately, he had been throwing more and more threats his way. I didn't know if that was because of how inefficient Lox was or because he just felt like he wasn't good enough for me. That was the one part I hadn't figured out yet.

"Yes, my child," he answered.

"The deal with the Youngs is set, and everything is in motion. They said by this time next year, I will be set for life both ways. I think this is really a good move for us. I hope everything goes as planned. I don't want to disappoint you on this, and I know a lot is riding on it," I told him.

I understood that this move would take us to a totally different level. Now, the Khan name rocked in the streets, but that was it. Working with Sage, we would have some visible assets and start to rock the business community. I was all for this move because I never really wanted to be in charge of the cartel in the first place.

"Everything will be fine. There is more riding on this than you know," he told me.

Before I could ask him what he was talking about, he ended the call. I guess I had been sitting outside for too long because there was a knock on my window. I looked up to see Markos and the other guy standing there waiting for me to roll the window down.

"You good? Do you need an escort home or something? You sitting out here on the phone like you arguing with fuck boy or something," Markos said.

I shook my head because I wasn't even acting like I was arguing. He was just being an asshole right now.

"I'm fine. I was just talking to my dad. Were you watching me?" I asked.

"Hell yeah. We working with you now, so that means that you are an investment to us. If you dead or all fucked up, how we gonna make you look legit for the crackers?" Markos said laughing.

He was a hard guy to understand, but he was growing on me. Even though he said some harsh shit, I know he meant well.

"I'm fine. Thanks for asking. I will see y'all at the next meeting, I guess," I said to them.

They nodded their heads, and I pulled out of the parking space. As I was driving out of the parking lot, I saw Sage in the window of his office looking down at us. I wondered why he didn't come down with them. It wasn't like he was busy because if he was, he wouldn't be standing there looking at me.

I sat in the back of the parking lot waiting for these niggas to go back in the building. Yeah, had I been following Nailah's sneaky ass for days now. She either didn't know or didn't care to know. I know she usually paid attention to her surroundings, but now she was being real fucking sloppy.

As the two niggas walked back into the building, the nigga, Sage, was standing in the window. He was too busy watching Nailah pull out to pay me any mind.

Those two had something going on. At the dinner, even though they were fussing, there was some other shit going on. I don't remember him saying much of anything to his fucking date. He was too busy beefing with Nailah to pay her any mind. Since I've been following her, I hadn't seen them together except for today, but I still say they're either fucking or about to be.

I followed her ass to the mall. Just my fucking luck she was going shopping today. Instead of going into the mall just to see her spend money, I decided to go check out Dee. I hadn't seen her since I started following Nailah's disloyal ass. I called up Dee to make sure her ass was home.

"Hello," she answered.

"I need you home and naked. I'm on my way," I told her.

"You must have the wrong number. I haven't heard from your black ass in how many days? You got life and me fucked up. I'm not home, and I'm not going home anytime soon," she fussed.

"You not home? How you get to where you are? You don't have a fucking car or a job. I don't care if it takes me a fucking month to call you, when I call, you better be wet, fresh, and naked!" I yelled at her.

She was getting on my fucking nerves with that bullshit. Knowing her ass was sitting at home on the fucking couch looking at fucking TV. She didn't do anything else. I think her ass is allergic to doing anything productive.

"Go to my house and see if I'm there then," she said in her smart ass tone.

This bitch ended the fucking call on my ass. I don't know why she made me act like that with her. I already had street shit on my mind. The last thing I needed was for my back-up to start acting up now. She didn't know I had the tracker on her phone, so I was about to have some face to face action with a nigga. I don't know who she was with, but the BBQ spot was gonna have some action in a minute. This bitch had me fucked up. I couldn't snatch up Nailah without my life being in danger, but Dee, her ass was about to get it.

It took me about fifteen minutes to get to the food spot. They looked like they were crowded, but that wasn't gonna stop me from snatching her ass up. I looked around once I walked in and saw her laughing and joking around with some of her bird ass friends. At least she wasn't there with a nigga. I walked over to the table and picked her ass up by her neck.

"What was that shit you was spitting on the phone?" I whispered in her ear.

All eyes were on us. Her little friends were beating on my back, but that didn't make me loosen my grip on her ass. She was clawing at my hands and trying to get me to loosen up.

"Let her fucking go, nigga. What the fuck is wrong with you?" her little friends yelled at me.

"You gonna bring your ass with me out of here. Do you fucking understand? You keep fucking with me, and I'm gonna find somebody to replace your option B ass. Keep fucking with me and find out what I do!" I yelled at her.

I let her go, and she coughed a little bit but got herself together, so she could follow me out the door. I was almost at the door when I heard someone call my name.

"Aye yo, Lox," the last nigga on earth that I needed to see said.

I saw him walking up to me. I was trying to look around and see who he was with, but I didn't see anybody.

"Sup, Markos? What are you doing on this side of town?" I asked.

I was trying to sound unbothered by him being there. I could tell by the way he looked at me that he wanted to say more, but he didn't.

"I followed somebody up here. Now, I'm just chilling and taking pictures of the scenery and shit. You know how it goes, right? You see some shit you might have to share with friends, and you just gotta take the pic. You know, to look at it later or throw it up on Snap Chat or some girly shit like that. You never know, my shit might end up on ShadeRoom one day. You know everybody wanna be famous," he said with a smirk.

Did this nigga just threaten my ass? He was standing there all calm and shit, but I could read between the fucking lines. His ass followed me up there and took fucking pics of my ass. His tone was nothing out of the ordinary, but it was his eyes that were telling the real story. This nigga was gonna be the one to fucking kill my ass. I was so pissed with Dee that I didn't even know that I was being followed.

I hated those niggas with a fucking passion. They walked around like they ran shit. I knew they did, but they didn't have to flaunt that shit like they did. I mean, they walked around like everybody was supposed to bow down to them. Markos and Sage weren't even in the streets, but it didn't matter because they had the last name Young. All those niggas needed to die. If they were out of the way, I could get out of the shadows of Nailah and her damn father.

He dapped me up and gave me a half of hug like we were cool or something.

"Tick, tock, motherfucker. That's for you and this bitch beside you," he said in my ear and walked away.

"Who was that, baby?" DeJa asked all loud and shit.

"Just get your shit and come on," I told her.

The whole ride, she asked question after question. She was fucking with my nerves so bad I finally had to shut her ass up.

"He knows my ole lady. Now shut the fuck up before I pull over on the interstate and let you call an Uber," I barked at her.

She kissed her teeth and mumbled some shit, but she kept that shit low enough that I couldn't make out what she said. I dropped her ass off, not even waiting for her feet to hit the ground before pulling off. I had to figure out what I was gonna tell Nailah because I knew that nigga called her as soon as he could.

Chapter Eight

8-DEJA

See, Lox thought he was doing something by threatening me while we were in the car. I had a trick for his ass. If that dude didn't tell princess Nailah what the deal was, I damn sure would. I knew he was gonna blame her finding out on me, so I might as well give him a reason to be mad. Let me explain some shit to y'all about Mr. Lox.

Lox and I have been together off and on for almost ten years. Yes, you read that right. Granted, we were broken up when he and Nailah started their so-called relationship. It didn't matter because he was always calling me and trying to get back with me. It was his idea to stay with her so he could take over completely. She was too dumb or too self-absorbed to see that he was sabotaging her shit. The problem with Lox is that he talked too damn much and didn't listen enough. He would talk big shit around people to make them think that he had more say so than he did. I'm sure the niggas under him knew the truth, but that didn't stop him from fronting every chance he got.

I changed my clothes and headed to Nailah's house. Yes, I knew where she lived. I even stayed at her house, cooked in her kitchen, and fucked my man in their bed when she was out of town. All of this is stuff I'm sure she didn't know about, but I hoped she was ready for the bombs I was about to drop on her ass. She could walk around like she was better than everyone all she wanted. I was gonna knock her ass down a notch or two on this day.

I drove down the street listening to Cardi B and getting myself hyped up. I knew she was gonna want to fight my ass, but I was ready for that shit too. I walked up to her door with an extra pep in my step, ready to ruin a bitch's day.

"How can I help you?" she asked.

"Yes, are you Nailah?" I asked, knowing damn well who she was.

"I'm guessing because I don't know you, but you somehow found your way to my door, that this has something to do with Lox. Come on in. You can help me pack his shit," she said.

She didn't even wait for me to say if I was helping her or not. She left the door wide open and went back into the house. She had Beyoncé blasting through the house. This bitch was too damn happy for me.

I walked into their bedroom, and she acted like she was just cleaning out her closet. There were no tears, no hurt, Mary J music, or none of that shit.

"Can you pass me the tape?" she asked.

I passed it to her and waited for her to cuss me out or something.

"Thanks," she said as she took the tape.

I watched her tape up a box then start packing another one.

"So, are you gonna say what you came knocking on my door for?" she asked me.

"Yeah, umm. I've been in a relationship with Lox for the past ten years off and on. I've stayed in your house, fucked in your kitchen, in your bed, and everything when you were gone on trips out of town. He told me that if he left you that your little illegal business would go down the drain. That's the main reason why he stayed with you. Not only that, but he's trying to take over all your shit and leave you broke," I told her.

She sat down at the foot of the bed. I was standing there on guard, waiting for her to jump up so we could get to knucking this shit out, but the bitch never got up.

"DeJa, let me explain some things to you, love," she said calmly.

How does she know my name? I never told her what my name was.

"Yes, I know who you are. I know your name, your address, even your social services case number. The thing is, you came here looking for a fight, or even an argument. The only thing you leaving here with is these boxes and some extra knowledge. I do want to set you straight on a few things though. First of all, there is nothing LITTLE about my business. Secondly, I will NEVER EVER be broke. I can tell from what you're saying that he has told you all the wrong shit. What he should have been telling you is that I can kill you with my bare hands or any gun that I choose depending on how I feel that day.

"You look a little confused, but there is no need to be. I know you came here without all the needed information. Now that you know, I hope this is the last time you knock on any of my doors. This is the only pass that you will get from me or anyone associated with me. I know you got that hood mentality, but just know that everybody ain't on that hood shit. I refuse to be fighting over a nigga with a ding-a-ling that refuses to fuck me like I want to be fucked," she said.

My phone rang. I looked down, and it was Lox. I wasn't going to answer the phone, but then Nailah said something.

"Go 'head and answer it. I'm sure there is a lie that he feels you need to hear," she said calmly.

"Hello," I answered with him on speakerphone.

"Hey, baby. I'm gonna be staying home with my girl for the next few days. I have to smooth this shit out with Nailah. I just wanted to give you a heads up," he lied so easily.

"I thought you were leaving her anyway, Lox?" I asked him.

"I am, but I gotta do this shit at the right time so I can fucking take over, then me and you can run shit," he explained.

Nailah seemed unfazed by everything he was saying. I mean, this bitch was still fucking packing. Not once did she ball up her face, smack her lips, or even roll an eye. She took unbothered to another level. I ended the call with him then she started talking again.

"You not the only OTHER one. Hell, I doubt if he ever dealt with one woman in his fucking life. I feel sorry for you because you out here putting your all into a man who clearly isn't that into anyone but his damn self," she told me.

I thought about what she was saying. I had come to her house to fuck up her day, but I was the one with tears in my eyes because of a man who I thought was mine. I turned to leave her house, but as I walked to the door, she called out to me.

"DeJa, you're leaving his boxes," she called out.

"Fuck him and his boxes," I told her just before closing her door.

Now it was time for me to find out where the hell Lox was and fuck up his day.

Chapter Nine

9 – MARKOS

*S*age, Montay and I were at Outback eating and talking. Those two may have been my cousins, but we were brothers, no doubt about it. We were always with each other growing up, went to school together, went to college together, we even fucked a few hoes together.

Sage was the darkest and the quietest of all of us. Me and Montay were more alike in that we didn't think about much that we said before we said it. We got out complexions from our fathers, so we both were brown skinned. Montay and Sage wore those big ass beards, trying to outdo James Harden and shit. It was funny as hell watching those niggas get their beards washed and all that shit. That shit just wasn't my thing. I didn't need anything in my way when I'm eating some pussy. I didn't eat everybody's pussy either, but I did have a couple in my rotation who got that type of pleasure from me.

"Can I get anything else for you gentlemen?" the waitress asked us with a smile.

"You can back up a little bit and get those damn titties and dirty ass shirt away from me," Montay said.

The chick looked so damn embarrassed when he said that shit, and we couldn't do shit but laugh at her ass. She had been acting all thirsty the whole time she was supposed to be serving us. You know how chicks get, laughing at nothing at all, overly talkative, and way too much movement trying to get us to look at her titties.

"Don't get all hush mouthed now. You done already flirted your way out of a tip. I got a question, though. Is one of them shits bigger than the other, or is your bra lopsided? Something just don't look right. You should really check into that shit. It looks unhealthy," Montay told her.

She slammed the bill down on the table and walked fast as hell away from the table.

"You know she gonna cry in the bathroom," I said.

"Man, fuck that broad and her lopsided titties. What's going on with Doll Baby? Did y'all tell her about our past yet?" Montay asked.

"No, I plan to do it, but how can I tell her we have that much history with each other? I'm trying to figure out why her father never told her. There has to be something more to what those old niggas are saying. Think about it. After all this time, why would her pops want a meeting with us now? It's been years. His money could have been cleaned up a long ass time ago," Sage said.

"Yeah, I was wondering about that too. Shit, I really want to know why she don't fucking remember us in the first damn place. I know we beat her ass enough for her to remember. She can only fight because of us in the first place. I'm going to drain the main vein. I'll be back," I told them.

Truthfully, there was more than that bothering me about this whole Doll Baby situation. I was thinking too fucking hard or something because I bumped into some chick who was holding a tray full of dirty dishes. The dishes fell, and some broke when they hit the floor, but there were some that slid across the floor. She didn't say a word, but she rolled her eyes before bending down to pick the dishes up.

"My bad, shawty," I told her as I bent down beside her.

"It's fine. You can go ahead and go where you were going. I'll get this up," she said. "Sir, I have it. It's no problem," she added as she looked up.

Shawty was beautiful. Although she looked tired as fuck, she was a sight to see even in her work uniform. She was in such a rush to pick up the broken pieces that she cut the palm of her hand.

"Fuck, got damn it," she cussed, holding her hand.

I grabbed one of the napkins off the closest table and wrapped it around the cut.

"You need to go to the hospital to get this checked out. It doesn't look good," I told her.

"I can't leave 'til my shift is over, so it's gonna have to wait," she said as she winced in pain.

"So, you gonna bleed ya little ass to death to keep ya fucking hours? You can't spend ya money if you dead, shawty, real shit. Get your ass up. I'll take you to the hospital," I told her.

"That's exactly what I need. Another fucking bill," she mumbled.

"Yo, real shit, bring ya ass. I'll talk to ya boss, and I'll pay ya hospital bill since I made you drop the shit in the first place," I told her.

She finally stopped fighting my ass and followed me to the car. I pulled my phone out so I could call my cousins to let them know what happened.

"You gotta call me from the bathroom?" Sage asked when he answered the phone.

"Real funny. I need you to go tell the manager that umm the girl that bus tables hurt her hand. I'm taking her to the emergency room since the shit is my fault. I'll bring her back when she done," I told him.

"The girl that bus tables? What's her name, nigga?" he asked.

I looked over at her, and she looked like she was in a lot of pain, so I hit the pedal a little harder. I saw what the name tag said, but that shit was weird as hell.

"Baltimore, that's her name, Baltimore," I told him.

"Her name is Baltimore? Really, nigga?" he asked.

"That's what her name tag says. So yeah, her fucking name is Baltimore. Just do that shit for me. I'll call you when I'm finished doing this," I told him before ending the call.

I could hear her sniffling as I sped through the streets. Her stubborn ass was sitting there crying, but she was gonna finish her whole shift. I shook my head at her ass.

"You gotta man or some kids that I need to call and let them know you got hurt on the job?" I asked.

"Nah, it's just me," she answered.

A few minutes later, we pulled up to the emergency room. I threw the car into park and jogged over to the passenger side of the car to open the door for her. She didn't want to act like she was in a lot of pain, but I knew she was. I scooped her up and walked her into the emergency department.

"I cut my hand, not my feet or legs," she told me.

"Just chill out and let me do me," I replied.

She shut her mouth, and I did what I had to do to get her back to the back.

"Aye, I need some help. My girl cut her hand and passed out." I winked my eye at Baltimore, and she laid her head on my shoulder with her eyes closed. I like that she paid attention and went with the flow.

"Where was she when this happened?" a nurse asked.

"She was at work. She cut her hand on a broken plate. It looks kind of deep too," I told her.

"Follow me. We have to get her looked at."

The lady led me to a room, and I laid Baltimore on the bed. Her eyes were still closed, but I could tell she wanted to laugh.

"Stay here with her while I go get something to try to wake her up and a doctor to look at her hand," she said as she rushed out the door.

When I looked to see that she was gone down the hallway, we both busted out laughing. Baltimore had a sense of humor and a nice smile. Her laugh was funny as hell too. I started to feel bad for making her drop the dishes in the first place.

"I'm sorry about causing all the shit that brought you here. I'm gonna cover your medical bills and your lost wages," I told her.

"Lost wages?" she asked.

She looked me up and down before she started talking again.

"What type of drug dealer are you that uses the words lost wages?" she asked.

"I'm a lawyer, nigga. What the hell made you think I was a drug dealer?" I asked her.

"You not dressed like any lawyer I've seen before. Are you a hood lawyer or a real lawyer?" she asked.

I pulled out one of my cards and gave it to her. She looked at it like something was wrong with it. This chick was funny.

"Markos Young, attorney at law," she read the card.

"Yup, that's ya boy. Any other questions?" I asked her.

The doctor and two nurses finally came in. They looked at her hand for a few minutes, then the doctor stitched her up. They gave her some potent pain pills and a doctor's note for five days out of work. We waited for her discharge papers, and once they came, I stood up to walk out the door.

"Markos, you not gonna carry me back to the car?" she asked with a smile on her face.

I scooped her up from the bed and carried her ass to the car. She was gonna learn not to ask me to do something because nine times out of ten I would do anything for her with no hesitation.

"Type your address into the GPS," I told her when I got in the car.

"I can direct you on where to go," she slurred.

"They just gave your ass the good shit. You'll be sleep before I make it to the highway," I told her.

A few seconds later, her ass was out just like I thought.

10 – BALTIMORE

"Shawty, we at your spot. You need me to check the house out for you? You all fucked up, so the worst you could do is kick a nigga in the knee or the shins if they come at you," he told me.

He always had some slick shit to say out his mouth. I wondered what it would be like to see him in action in the courtroom. He looked like he was one of those guys who were nothing but tears and nights of worry for the female in his life.

I'm Baltimore, I don't know why my mom named me that. I had never been to Baltimore, and I didn't have any desire to go either. I'm twenty-five years old, and I stand five feet three, brown skin. Not skinny, but not thick either. I work my ass off to pay for my apartment. I'm not on any type of state assistance, so in order for me to eat, keep the lights on, keep some food in the house, and keep my cell bill paid, I had to work. Which is why even with these stitches in my hand and a doctor's note, I'm taking my ass to work tomorrow. I'm gonna have to work a double to make up for the time I lost tonight.

"Give me your keys," he told me.

"Why? I can walk, and I have a whole hand that I can use to

open the door. I appreciate all your help, but I got it from here," I told him.

Markos cut the car off and hopped out the car. Those pills that the hospital gave me had my ass high as hell right now. I walked up to the door and fumbled with the keys until they were snatched out of my hand. He opened the door for me and stepped inside. I stood in the doorway watching him walk through my apartment like he was looking for somebody.

"What are you doing?" I asked him.

"You know when you get off late at night like I know you do, you should leave a light on. It's not a good look coming to a dark house after a long day at work. I had to search and make sure no hard-headed nigga was in here," he told me.

He walked into my kitchen and opened the fridge. I came on into the apartment then closed and locked the door behind me.

"Shawty, you ain't got shit in here to eat. What you gonna eat tonight?" he asked.

"I'm gonna fix a sandwich then go to bed. Why? Why are you still here?" I asked him.

"I'm spending the night so I can take you to get your car in the morning from your job," he told me.

"I don't have a car, so you can leave," I told him.

He stopped what he was doing and looked at me like I had confused him. He looked around then he sighed, slid his hands into his pockets, and leaned against the empty but closed refrigerator.

"How the fuck you get to work?" he asked.

"I walk."

"You walk to work? So, you walk home too?" he asked.

"Yeah, unless one of the girls gives me a ride home," I told him.

"What's ya story, Baltimore? You not rachet from what I can tell. You obviously work your ass off, and you're struggling to stay above water, but you're not bitter. So, how you get here? Where your people?" he asked.

I walked to the fridge, waited for him to move his tall, lanky ass out of the way then poured me some soda in one of the red plastic cups on the counter. I sat down on the couch, and I didn't have to look up to know that he was staring at me. I could feel his eyes on me like they were laser beams.

"I work and come home, that's it. As long as I keep my bills paid, I'm fine. I'm not out here stripping or doing anything illegal to make money, so I'm not complaining. I see the girls out here selling their souls for a head full of weave and a name brand bag filled with overdue bills," I told him.

I knew from the outside looking in it looked like I was barely making it. Maybe the way I was living check to check wasn't all that life had to offer. For now, I was satisfied with how I was making it. It was hard, no doubt about it, but it was nothing that I couldn't handle.

"I like your fucking hustle, shawty. Your shit is official as fuck. I'm gonna make a few calls and get some food delivered to ya twice a month. Tomorrow, when we get up, we're gonna go find you a nice little whip so your ass can stop walking to work," he said like it was nothing.

"I'm not a charity case or no shit like that. I don't need that kind of help. People just don't go around helping people with groceries and cars, so what's your angle? Are you a pimp on the side? You want me to be your side bitch or something? Or are you just always playing Captain-Save-A-Bitch every day of the week except Sundays?" I asked.

I hated to be looked at as a fucking charity case or someone looking for a handout. I worked for my shit, so nobody could come and tell me what they've done for me.

"I'm not captain save nobody, and you not a charity case, so miss me with the bullshit. You can bitch and moan all night. I'm gonna do what I said for you regardless. I'm staying here with you. I know your stubborn ass will go to work even though you got a doctor's note. Go 'head and get ya ass in the shower so you can take your ass to bed. I'm gonna lay on this damn couch. See you in the morning, shawty," he said.

I took my shower and tried to sleep, but the pain from my hand kept me up most of the night. I lay across my bed watching the sun rise. I got up and moved around my room, making sure not to make any noise. I didn't need the warden to wake up so he could stop me from going to work. I held my shoes in my hand as I creeped slowly down the hallway. He was lying on the couch just like he said he would last night. I almost got to the door before I heard him clapping his hands. I stopped and dropped my head because I knew there was no way I was going to work today.

"You hardheaded as fuck. I guess that means your ass is soft," he said.

I stayed facing the door. I didn't want to turn around, but I knew I had to.

"You don't have shit to eat in here, so we going to get some breakfast since you up and all that good shit," he said.

"I'm going to work. I can't afford to take off even with a messed-up hand. It's gonna set me back like a mother fucker," I told him.

"Put your shoes on before we go out the door. It's country as fuck to walk outside with no shoes on. Ladies don't curse a lot either, so you gonna have to work on that. Come on, I gotta stop by one of my spots. I can't be walking around looking like yesterday," he said.

It was amazing to me how he waited for me to stop talking, but he paid no mind to anything I said. I was wasting my breath with him.

I shook my head and put my shoes on. We walked to his car, and he opened the door for me. At least he was a gentleman. He had selective hearing, but he was a gentleman nonetheless. He hopped in the driver's seat and started the car.

"You know I don't care about you sitting over there pouting like you two years old and shit, right?" he asked me.

I kissed my teeth and rolled my eyes at him then I looked out the window while he drove. He would occasionally glance in my direction just to laugh. This was going to be the longest day ever.

Chapter Eleven

11- NAILAH

I was sitting in the living room when the president of the community dick club decided to bring his ass in the house. I was chilling and not paying him any mind. He walked in the bedroom, and I could hear the drawers opening and closing. His heavy ass boots were stomping across the floor.

"Where the fuck is my shit?" he asked with a raised voice.

"Oh, so you did see me sitting here," I said.

"How the fuck can I not? Where is my shit, Nailah?" he asked again.

"They should be at your brother's house by now. I did pay the guy a little extra to take the long route, though," I told him.

"What the fuck? You could have said that shit when I came in here. You fucking tripping now. Call whoever dude is so he can bring my shit back," he fussed.

"DeJa wants you to call her," I told him.

His face looked like he had seen a ghost. His rah-rah demeanor had gone away just that quick.

"Who?" he asked.

"DeJa. You know DeJa, she's the one you talked to not that long ago. You know, you told her that you were gonna be home with me for the next few days. The only problem was that while you were telling her that you were with me. She was standing in the doorway of my room watching me pack your shit. Poor thing was all torn up when she figured out that she wasn't the only 'other' chick in your life," I told him.

I laughed and went to the kitchen to get some wine. This bullshit that was going on deserved a toast.

"I don't know what she told you, but she lied. I would never cheat on you," he pleaded.

"Since she told me you and her were together for ten years, you're absolutely right. I was the other woman because we damn sure haven't been together that long," I told him.

I knew he was wondering why I was so calm, but hey, why keep trying to force a nigga to do right? I shook my head at him. I just couldn't understand why he even wanted to take over so bad. He wasn't the true savage type. He wasn't too bright, but hey, he could play with fire if he wanted to.

"Bitch, you can stand there with that stupid ass smirk on your face all you want. You forget I know your operation inside out. I can shut shit down and make you bleed out here in these streets," he said.

I took a sip from my wine glass, being sure not to take my eyes off him the whole time. This was what I meant by he didn't have what it takes. Did he honestly think that I would hear him say all that shit on the phone and keep shit the same? There is no way he could think that I was kicking his ass out, but he was still gonna run my shit. I picked up my phone and sent a text. I needed to get out of this house before I killed this nigga. It would be a shame too because the community thots and tricks would lose their gravy train. I was all about giving back to the community, so that's where his ass was going.

"Let me find out you over there texting them Young niggas. I know you fucking one of them. I wouldn't be surprised if you not busting that four-car garage sized pussy open for all them niggas. Shit so fucking loose you gotta keep ya legs closed for me to even feel some of the lining of that overused shit," he said.

He really expected me to react to the dumb shit he was saying. My pussy was tight as a motherfucking virgin. He was just pissed because he saw that I wasn't playing with his ass. There was a knock on the door, which made me smile because shit was about to get interesting.

He walked his wanna play angry ass to the door. Yes, I let him because it was for his ass anyway. While he opened the door, I turned the TV off and gathered up my purse and keys. I also took my house, cars, safety deposit box, and post office box keys off his key ring.

"What the fuck this big nigga Moose doing here? Oh, you couldn't be woman enough to put my ass out, so you had to call ya daddy's muscle man over here. You ain't nothing but a weak ass little girl in a bad bitch's body," he said.

I knew he had more to say, but Moose had snatched his ass up like he was a newspaper in the driveway. His legs were moving all fast, trying to get a solid footing on the floor. Moose just tossed his ass off the porch like he was Jeffery from The Fresh Prince. He was yelling and cussing like there was no tomorrow.

"I called you an Uber. The car you were driving has my name on it, so it stays here. Your cell phone is in my name, so that shit is off," I told him from behind Moose.

"You dirty bitch. I'm gonna get your ass for this, you watch and see. Daddy's not gonna be around to save your vindictive ass then. Watch and see," he said.

I watched him get himself together before he took off walking down the street.

"You gon' be straight, Nailah? You know I gotta tell ya pops about this," Moose said.

I just nodded my head because I knew this was only the beginning.

"Who is that?" Moose asked.

I looked up to see Sage pulling up. This nigga had some hellified timing. He got out of the car with a curious look on his face.

"Why ya man walking down the street? What's up, Big Moose?" Sage said when he walked up to us.

I didn't know he knew Moose, but I guess I shouldn't be surprised. Moose looked like he wanted to say or ask something, but he just walked away.

"I have a meeting to get to. You wanna ride with me? Just to observe me on my Boss Beauty shit. I had to shut shit down for two weeks. I found out Lox was trying to take my shit from under me. I have his phone records, so now it's time to cut the snakes from my shit," I said to Sage.

"You want me to drive? You know I'm not gonna let you do this shit on ya own. Them niggas might wanna jump stupid or something. You ready now or what?" he asked.

I went to lock the door, and we headed out.

∞∞∞∞∞∞∞∞

"Lox is no longer a part of this organization. If he comes around, nothing about this organization is to be discussed. Now, on to the next issue. Which one of y'all have been working with him to take over?" I asked.

I knew that the question caught some of them by surprise, but I noted the ones who had no look of surprise or confusion. Sage and I looked at each other. I guess he was thinking the same thing that I was.

"Who the fuck are you, though? We ain't never seen you before, yet you in here running ya mouth. No introductions or nothing," some nigga said.

I went to my purse and pulled out my gun. I aimed it and shot him in the head. Everyone in the room jumped, even Sage.

"Is there anyone else who has questions about who I am?" I asked.

No one said anything, so I put my gun back in my purse. I

smoothed out my burgundy pencil skirt then walked around to the front of the desk and leaned against it.

"I'm the woman who has been running this organization for the last seven years. Lox was my puppet, so to speak. The orders and moves that he made were only made because I told him what to say and how to move. As you just saw, I have no problem killing any of y'all. I have no issue with any of you yet..." I stopped what I was saying.

I forgot I had the phone records in my purse. I took them out along with a burner phone. I dialed the first number that was dialed way too much on Lox's phone records. I had the names of every phone number that was on the list. I just called the male numbers because he nor his bitches were no longer my concern. The phone rang just like I knew it would.

"If your phone rings can you go stand on the other side of the room. I'm just trying to clear some things up," I said.

As I continued to call the numbers, just like I asked, they all walked over to the other side of the room. Once I was done calling the phone numbers, it was time for me to make my point.

"Now, gentlemen, I know that you feel some type of way because a female is calling the shots. I don't want anyone to get confused about my position. I'm the boss, no way around it. I will show you the same respect and loyalty you show me. Now if you show me disloyalty and disrespect, I will show you death. No need to explain or try to plead your case. Know that if I approach you, I already have the answers I need. No one will ever take my curves, bra size, shoe fetish, or the fact that I bleed once a month to say that I'm weak or unfair," I told them.

The ones on the other side of the room were looking nervous. They looked like they wanted to say something. I ignored them because at this time my patience was running thin, and I was hungry. I chose a few niggas from the other side and lined them up facing the snakes. I stood with them all lined up.

"Take out your guns and aim them at the person in front of you. The person in front of you is a snake. They were trying to take food out of you and your family's mouth. They were easily manipulated by a nigga who didn't have a mind of his own. A nigga who felt like he was better than all of you when he was really just the one fucking the boss. That right there warrants a death sentence. Don't worry, fellas, I'm standing right here with y'all. We can build a family on loyalty and respect. If you kill with me, I will kill with you. Let's get these niggas out of here so I can go eat," I said.

We all aimed our guns and pulled the trigger. The bodies dropped like dominoes. I turned to them to speak my last piece.

"I promise not to let my pussy make decisions from here on out. Can y'all promise not to let your dicks get you killed?" I asked.

They all nodded in agreement.

"You all will find an envelope in each of your cars. Take that money and have fun on your vacation. Shop is closed for two weeks. Make sure you're ready to grind when we open up shop because we're gonna be working around the clock. Enjoy your vacations, gentlemen," I told them.

I walked out of the door winking my eye at Sage. I almost forgot he was with me. He gave me his smirk and walked out with me. I never wanted to run this shit, but since I had no other choice, I might as well own it like the Boss Beauty that I am.

Chapter Twelve

12 – SAGE

*S*eeing her in action kind of pissed me off. She was built for this shit. I see why her pops really chose her. It wasn't because of her being the only child either. I knew that he and my pops were up to some shit for real now. There was something off about this whole shit. I was in the car driving to get us something to eat. I knew she felt like I was mad at the way she was moving because I was quiet as fuck right now. I wasn't, but I was trying to figure out what was going on.

"Do you mind if we just go to my place? I can get my chef to whip you up something," I asked her.

"I don't mind as long as you don't kill me while we're there," she said.

"Yo, on some real shit. I know your little boyfriend was a snake, but don't ever come at me like that. If I was gonna kill you, I would have done that the first day you walked your ass in my office. I will never be disloyal or a fucking snake. If I don't fuck with you, then I don't fuck with you. You shouldn't go around accusing people of shit because you don't know a snake when you see one. I bet his snake ass could eat the fuck outta some pussy too, huh?" I asked her.

I know I might've hurt her little feelings, but she betta

recognize I'm not that nigga. She could be the boss of her crew all day long, but when we together, I run shit. I decided that I needed her help. I just hoped she didn't freak out when I told her how connected we really were.

Once we got to the house, I let the chef know that he would be making dinner for two. He looked at me funny, but that was because I never brought anyone to that house before. I told him it was a female, and his old ass started moving around the kitchen like he was on some energy drinks or something. I took Nailah outside in the back so we could talk.

"Your backyard is beautiful. I would be out here more than in the house if I lived here. You could have some parties back here," she said.

She was walking around the yard with a big smile on her face. My yard was my little project when I first moved here. Now it had a flowing waterfall. The water fell into a man-made pond filled with exotic, colorful fish. There was a pool with a warmer, and fluorescent lights that were on a timer. When I had time, I would come out there and sit for hours. This was my space to sit in silence. My days were bombarded with meeting after meeting, helping person after person. This was my peace in my world of chaos.

"Sit over here with me. We have to talk," I told her.

She came over and sat with me by the pool. The lights dancing across her skin was a fucking beautiful sight. Her phone rang, but she ignored the call.

"Nailah, do you remember coming to your dad's friend's house when you were little? He had his sons and nephews over there with him all the time. They used to beat you up and harass you all the time. They called you Doll Baby," I told her.

"Wait a minute there was this one boy, and he would always fight the other ones when they picked on me. I remember, but that was ages ago. I wasn't even ten years old yet. Wow! Do you know them? I wonder what they're doing now," she said.

I looked at her and shook my head. Then I took my phone

out and showed her the picture. She looked at me and back at the phone.

"H-how did you get this?" she asked.

"That's me, Markos, and Montay," I told her as I pointed to us in the picture.

"That's why I feel so comfortable around y'all. Y'all were like my brothers back then. But, wait a minute, why didn't daddy tell me who you guys were? How's your dad doing? It was like after my mom left, I never saw y'all again," she said.

She was talking so fast that I had to laugh at her. I could see the excitement in her eyes.

"What did your dad tell you about coming to us for help?" I asked.

"He just said that it was time to think outside the box. I agreed with him, so I didn't question it. I'm all for making the money work for us and grow. He was pissed that I let Lox meet with y'all first. He just kept saying that it wasn't his place," she said.

"I didn't even know who you really were until my dad told me. We haven't seen each other in ages. I didn't know your mom left. Where is she now?" I asked.

"I don't know. I came home from camp one summer, and my dad said that mom had left us. Me and her weren't that close because she always said I was a daddy's girl, which I definitely am, and it's always been that way. I never really thought too much of her leaving because all my friends' parents were divorcing back then. Just after she left, I would bring her up, but once I stopped bringing her up, my dad acted like she never existed," she said.

It was crazy because my dad never said anything about her mom leaving. I remember her mom. She was more beautiful than her daughter. I had a little boy crush on her for the longest. She was my Vanity or Apollonia. I would just stare at her until she left the room, or my dad popped me upside my head.

"Have you talked to your mom?" I asked her.

"I haven't seen or heard from my mother since I left for camp that summer she left," she said sadly.

I felt a stinging sensation in my chest. She was a grown sexy woman, but right now, her eyes showed a lost little girl. This was my first time seeing her so vulnerable. She let a few tears fall, but that was it. I knew her father had groomed her never to show emotion, but there were some things that you can't control. She wasn't a machine, and she didn't have a cold heart. She was just a scared woman who didn't want to disappoint daddy. The thing that bothered me the most out of all of this is that I knew her father was holding out on her. I just hoped whatever it was that he was holding didn't break her to the point that she would turn into the cold-hearted bitch I think her father wanted her to be.

∞∞∞∞∞∞

"Pops isn't telling us the whole story. I don't even thing Nailah's pops is telling her the whole thing either. I asked her about her mom last night. She was all broke up about it. She was all sad and shit. Took me back to our younger days when she used to need us to protect her from the asshole white boys that lived down the street," I told Montay.

"Did you ask ya pops what was going on? I know he knows something. Think about it. You and Markos been doing this shit for years. Why does Khan need help now? Why would he send Nailah to come do it for him? He could have just sent the info to Pops and got him to tell y'all what to do. If you ask me, all them old heads know what's going on. They not gonna tell y'all, though. If her Pops never liked Lox, why wouldn't he have his ass killed? He could have made it look like an accident or even a hit, but he never did. I bet you any fucking thing that he knew that nigga was trying to take her shit from under her nose. He never stepped in, though. I'm all for tough love, but if a nigga is coming for my only child I'm killing his ass," Montay said.

"Lox is a fuck up, though. I'm surprised that he hasn't gotten himself killed since he and ol' girl broke up. There has to be somebody behind him," I replied.

"You're gonna have to talk to him. See if he can let you know what's going on," Montay said.

I knew that already, but the question was if Dad was gonna tell me the damn truth or not. He was always wanting to teach us something growing up. There was always a test, and I hoped this wasn't the case because it was time for him to learn that I'm not a damn child.

Chapter Thirteen

13 – POPS

*L*et me speak up for a minute. I'm Sage's father. I'm a low-key type of guy. Yes, I'm one of the founding members of the Young Cartel. I started all this shit. I never thought it could grow into what it was now. My brothers and I were sitting on millions of dollars. I know you already heard a little bit about my family's business, but, there's more.

Sage and my nephew, Markos, were the only legit members of the family. The rest of us were forehead deep in all types of illegal shit. Running guns, drugs, robbing little niggas on the street, chopping up cars, we were even selling fucking yachts. Around the time the boys were in high school, my brothers and I all agreed that we needed people on our team who were going to be loyal to the family no matter what. We all raised our kids on loyalty to family above all else. Once the boys graduated from law school and passed the bar, we let go of the money hungry lawyers we had on retainer.

I was especially proud of those two. They were making the Young name ring bells in the community and in business circles. Sage was more like me than he would care to admit, but that day will come soon enough. Now getting to the point instead of rambling, Geronimo and I came up in this shit together. Him having access to people out of the country was a help to us both. With his connections and our manpower, we took over the seven cities like a mom takes a bottle from a baby. I admit that once we did get established and well known in the streets, the bullshit came with it.

Geronimo and Nailah were always at the house back when we were still establishing the status that we have now. All of our kids had been around each other so much that you would have thought they were all brothers and sisters. The boys protected the girls with no hesitation, no matter what was going on at the time. This alone is the reason Geronimo and I agreed that it was time to reconnect Nailah with my boys. Nailah had major shit goin on right under her nose, but she never took the time to be involved with her father's business. Geronimo knew that just coming to Nailah and telling her what was going on wasn't going to work. Nailah would feel like she was slipping or that her father was coming down on her for no reason.

The bullshit that I'm speaking of is centered around Lox and Leslie. Yes, I know the bitch's name. She's fucking a nigga that my seed created, so it was my duty to know everything about the bitch. I always acted like I couldn't remember her name just to fuck with Sage. It started out as a joke. I just kept doing it trying to see if he would catch on to the fact that Leslie wasn't the one for him. She was with him for the status of the Young name. I can say that she wasn't a gold digging tramp because she came from money. She just wanted to be hood royalty, and that's what the Young name provided. They were both just going through the motions now. When a relationship gets to the point that you two are never home together unless it's absolutely necessary, then there is a problem

Sage was a focused and determined young man. He was driven to be the best accountant that he could be. That means he had long hours at the office and longer hours away from Leslie. She would stay home and relax as long as he wasn't there. He told me of the many nights he would come home just to see her walk by dressed to impress for the club. She didn't cook, clean, or anything else a woman should do. I didn't ask about what kind of sex she was giving him because I already knew the answer to that. If a man is happy and satisfied with the sex his old lady is giving him, then he makes sure to take his ass home.

I wanted Sage to have the kind of love his mother and I had before she died. The same love that Geronimo and Nailah's mother had before she left. He couldn't do that until he found a woman who had his body and mind gone. Leslie only had that niggas weight gone from her not being the woman that he needed.

There was a knock at the door that brought me out of my thoughts. I went to get the door, and imagine my surprise when I saw Geronimo Khan standing there.

"Well damn, I didn't think you would come here. What's the occasion, motherfucker?" I asked him.

"Still the same asshole you've always been. I see some things never change. Are you going to invite me in, or do we have to talk out here?" he asked me.

I stepped to the side and let him in. When I looked him over, I was pleased with what I saw. He was still the same Geronimo. There were a few gray hairs here and there, but other than that and a little weight, he was still the same. I led him into my office and offered a drink and a cigar, which he declined. I could tell by the look he had that whatever he came for was something major. He looked around my office and saw all the pictures of the children along with a few of all of us.

"It's hard to believe you have all these pictures still hanging up in here. I guess I shouldn't be surprised. You always preached about the importance of family and loyalty," he said.

"You can't choose the people you are some kin to, but family is always chosen with care," I told him.

He nodded his head. That was one of the sayings that we used to use back in the day. There could be people with the same blood as you, but they could be the first ones coming for you.

Back in the day, Geronimo and my brothers were all I needed. He was one of us as if he came out of my mother's pussy just like we did.

"What's the deal?" I asked.

"I need you to find Nadia," he said.

"What the fuck you mean find her? Where the hell did you leave her body?" I asked.

He looked at me as if he didn't know what I was talking about. I shook my head because this shit was about to go left real quick. I hated liars and sneaky mother fuckers. Right now, I saw Geronimo as being both of those things.

"Body? What the hell you talking about? I didn't kill Nadia, nigga," he said.

He sat up in the seat and looked me in the eye. That wasn't enough for me right now. I needed more if I was going to believe him.

"You had to do something to her. I mean y'all were here all lovey dovey and shit, then you call talking about you can't find her. You never called crying or upset. Every time I saw you, you never mentioned shit about her, so I figured you killed her ass. That's the reason I stopped fucking with you like that," I told him.

"I love Nadia with all my heart. You know that. How the hell could you even think some shit like that about me? I haven't been right since she left. I cried many nights but, not in front of anybody. How the hell would that look? I'm supposed to be some hard ass, feared kingpin out here in the streets. You know me just like you know your brothers. It's fucked up that you weren't man enough to come to me about this. We been through shit that we agreed would never be discussed, but you couldn't come ask me about this? We've cut up dope, sold it, even killed some mother fuckers together before. You fucking know me, man," Geronimo said.

He looked like he was hurt that I could even think that about him killing his wife.

"For her to just up and disappear, the shit didn't seem right," I told him.

"It doesn't fucking matter if it seemed right or not. We're fucking brothers. That should have fucking mattered enough for you to open ya damn mouth. Instead, you around here acting like a bitch making assumptions and shit. I only came to you because you have a farther reach than I do. I need to find her to get an explanation of why she left like that. Nailah needs her mother too. She's gonna be the next queen pin out here. I need her to be that without giving up her feminine side. I can teach her, but if I continue to, she's gonna move like a man. I don't need that because if she starts doing it for too long, she might end up being a lesbian or something. I need some grandkids before I die," Geronimo said.

Leave it up to his ass to say all that together like what he just said was normal. How is Nailah going hard in the streets gonna make her a lesbian? He needs to cut the bullshit. With Nailah being around Sage again on the regular, they may just get together like they belong. Since they were children, they've always had a special connection. Maybe them working together can benefit all of us.

"I got a question. Why didn't you kill that nigga Lox?" I asked.

Shit, I needed to know. Since he was in the spill ya guts type of mood today, I was gonna use it to my benefit. Lox should have never been allowed to live as long as he has. I know there has to be a reason.

"Regardless of how useless Lox is, Nailah loves him. He's a fraud, punk, and a fucking leach, but she loves him. I know that if I kill him like I want to, it could break my little girl. I will be the first one that she blames for his death. The love she has for him lets me know that if I kill him, she will never forgive me. She's all I have left. I can't lose her, and especially not behind that wandering dick motherfucker," he explained.

I nodded my head because it did make sense even if I didn't like it.

"I'll help you, but if I find out you had anything to do with Nadia's disappearance, we're gonna have a fucking problem," I told Geronimo.

"Fuck you and your problem. I didn't kill her, nigga. How many fucking times do I have to say that shit?" he asked me.

I didn't respond because if I did then we would go back and forth all damn day. I know it took a lot for him to come here and ask me to help. Geronimo was as prideful as they come. That's one of the reasons that he started in this drug shit with us. He was too fucking broke to eat, and he didn't want to beg mother-fuckers for shit. So, the fact that it took him years of looking himself before coming to me didn't surprise me at all. I just hoped what I find doesn't cause our friendship to end.

Chapter Fourteen

14 – GERONIMO

I can't believe he thinks I killed Nadia. All this time I thought he was pissed because of me branching off and doing my own thing. I guess we were both wrong as fuck. Knowing that Pops had agreed to look for Nadia, it was now time to sit down with Nailah and let her know what was really going on.

When I pulled up into my circular driveway, I was surprised to see her car parked. She never came over and let herself in even though she had a key. I took a deep breath because I knew this would be a hard conversation to have. When I walked in the house, I saw Nailah sitting on the floor Indian style. She had taken out the box of old photos I had hidden away in my office closet.

"Why didn't you tell me that the Youngs were the boys I used to play with all the time? They were the brothers I never had back then. Sage wouldn't let anyone do anything to me. If one of the boys hit me or something he would always make them stand there while I hit them back. I didn't realize who they were until Sage brought up all those old memories tonight. Do you really know what happened to my mother? There had to be a reason why she just up and left like that," Nailah said.

"I knew you would figure out the connection you had with the Youngs sooner or later. You and Sage were the closest out of the group, though. You had a connection with each other that couldn't be explained. I have no idea what happened to your mother. In fact, I just come from seeing Pops Young, and he agreed to look for her," I told her.

"Fuck him. Why aren't you out there looking for her? Why did you wait this long to start looking for her? It's been well over twelve years, and now you want to call in favors?" she argued.

"The Youngs and I go way back. I'm talking about the dial-up internet was in full effect when we started," I said.

"You should have told me, Daddy. You had me going out here blind. You have no right to lie on my mother the way you did. I thought she left because I was too much for her. I sat up most nights praying for her to come back, but she never did," Nailah said.

"Like I said, I don't know where your mother is. She left to go get her nails and toes done, but she never came back. Her car, phone, clothes, and smile were never seen or heard of again. I went to file a missing person's report, but she had to be gone for 48 hours before they stepped in to do anything. I did go back to file an official report, but there were no leads in the case. That's when I hired a private investigator. I've been paying them to try to hunt her down ever since. Every time no information is found it's like she fell off the face of the earth, but I can feel it in my soul that she's still alive," I told her.

"You could have told me," she pleaded.

"Tell you for what? So, I can see you sitting here looking like a lost puppy? Seeing you looking sad breaks my heart, but not having your mother here with us has broken my soul," I revealed.

Hearing those words come out of my mouth hurt me more than Nailah would ever know. All these years I've been living as a shell of the man I was before. Nadia was my everything. Actually, she still is. I had a gift for her for all the important days that she had missed. Birthdays, Valentine's, Anniversaries, Mother's Day, and Christmas, I still shopped as if she was here with us. I was sure to put the year on each gift so she could open them in order. I woke up in the morning and still said good morning to her out loud as if she could hear me. My life didn't just revolve around her, but she was a major part of what gave me the motive to live.

I needed her here with me. No other woman would do. I hadn't given these women out here nothing more than a wet ass. It took me almost a year before I even looked at another woman. I knew in my heart that she wasn't gone because she wanted to be. There was a reason she was taken away from me, and I needed to find out what it was and who took her.

"Daddy, I could have helped you try to find her," Nailah said.

"It's not your place to help me find her. It's my fault she's gone in the first place. Just like it's my fault that she's been gone for so long. I just want to hear her voice again, see her smile, or smell her hair. Enough about that, tell me about the situation with you and Lox," I said.

"There is no Lox and I, so there is no situation. I put him out and switched up the houses, codes, routes, and other things that he might use against us," she told me.

"You not going to tell me the rest?" I asked her.

I knew all about her killing the guys at the meeting. Even though I understood her thoughts behind it, I was uncomfortable with it. I never wanted her to have to resort to killing people with her own hands. Killing someone is not a feeling that you ever get used to no matter how much they deserve it. She did it to ensure that her team would know how she gets down, but with that came a burden that she didn't need.

"Why would I tell you if you already know?" she asked.

"I don't want you out here trying to get a body count just to make these niggas out here respect you. You are a queen. A queen never gets her hands dirty or breaks a sweat. You need to figure out another way to earn their respect. There will come a time when your gun can't. They only put fear in the niggas who don't know any better. Once you run into the real bosses, they will dare you to pull the trigger. If you pull it, be ready for the shit storm that will follow. Real bosses are always connected. When you kill one or even attempt to pull a gun on one, there will always be consequences," I told her.

I looked her in the eye and prayed that she was listening to every word I said. It was times like these that I needed her mother. She could explain this shit to her in a way that made sense. I could only tell her how a man saw things. Everybody knows that men and women look at the same shit but see two different things.

"Daddy, I know all that, but the action fit the audience I had. They understood that the new boss wears six-inch pumps," she said with a smile on her face.

"Don't get too relaxed, Nailah. Keep an eye out for Lox because he's gonna come for you. You fucked up his name in the streets by taking over, and you hurt his ego by giving him his walking papers. Always stay alert, baby girl. Be careful as if your life depends on it because it does," I told her.

I gave her a kiss on her forehead and left her sitting on the couch. My day was long, and I needed to rest. I lay on the bed thinking about what my life would have been like if Nadia was with us. The phone rang, I looked at the clock. It read two-thirty in the morning. It had been years since I got a phone call like that. Going against my first thought, I answered the phone.

"Hello," I answered.

"Make sure that bitch has a bulletproof wig on," a male voice said.

"Who the hell is this?" I asked, sitting straight up in the bed.

"The nigga that's gonna kill your princess," he said before the line went dead.

I hopped out of bed and grabbed the clothes that were closest to me. I ran out the door to my car. Speeding down the highway, the only thing I could think about was somebody killing my daughter. She was all I had left. There was no way I could just stand by and let someone kill her. I pulled up to her house, and the car wasn't in the driveway like usual, and all the lights were out. I got out anyway just to be sure that she wasn't home.

"Nailah, Nailah!" I called out.

"Daddy, what are you doing here?" she asked, coming down the hallway.

"I need you to put some clothes on. We have to go somewhere," I told her.

Nailah didn't waste time arguing. I made a few phone calls while she was putting clothes on. She came running out dressed in all black with a black hood on her head. I almost laughed at her because she was dressed like she was going to rob somebody.

"We're not robbing anybody tonight," I told her.

"You never said what we were going to do, so I had to be prepared for anything," she explained.

She was right, but it was still a little bit funny. We rode in silence. It wasn't for long with me going damn near eighty miles an hour.

"Why are we here?" she asked.

I said nothing, but she was sure to follow my lead without voicing any more objections. We walked in the house, and of course, everyone had concerned looks on their faces. Once everyone was seated, I didn't waste any time, I immediately got to the point.

"There's been a threat made on my daughter's life. I know that we could easily hire a guard for her, but I'm not too sure of where this threat is coming from. I want her to be protected by family," I told everyone.

"Daddy, what the hell? You didn't say anything about a threat on my life," she said.

Pops, Sage, Markos, Montay were all looking at me. They could look confused all they wanted, but they were the only ones that I trusted with my baby's life.

"She can come stay with me," Sage said.

I knew he would be the one. He always looked out for her

when they were little kids. I knew that right now it wouldn't be any different, especially with her life in danger.

"Don't you have Leann there with you?" Pops asked.

"Leslie, Pops, her name is Leslie. And no, she has her own place," Sage answered.

"Fuck her and her name. I know if she comes at Doll Baby wrong, I will fuck her up. Don't put her in no shit that you can't control. If she's gonna be at your house, then you gotta kick that bitch to the curb. I would never hit a woman, but I will cuff her ass up and toss her across the street. You can't put Nailah in that situation," Pops said

"I got it, Pops," Sage told him.

"What?" Nailah asked.

"I said I got it. You can stay at the house with me. I only have to be in the office for meetings and shit. I can do all my other shit from the crib. Why the fuck everybody looking at me like that?" Sage said.

"Watch ya damn mouth, nigga. Make sure that Liza girl knows better than to try me. I'm not for the bullshit," Nailah said.

"Now here you go with the bullshit," Sage said.

15 – SAGE

"Y ou can choose any room to chill out in. Don't worry, every room has a bathroom. I'll take you by your spot tomorrow to pick up some clothes and whatever else you need," I told Nailah.

She's been quiet since we left my pop's house. I was sure she was still thinking about the fact that somebody was threatening her life. Eventually, she'd tell me what's on her mind. She didn't have any other choice.

There was a knock on the door, which I knew I probably shouldn't answer, but I answered it anyway.

"What you doing here?" I asked Leslie.

"I didn't know I needed a reason to see my man," she said.

I was going to tell her to kick rocks, but instead, I let her in. I know I was being petty as fuck right now, but hey, I wanted to know how this shit turned out.

"I haven't heard from you. Is there something you need to tell me?" she asked.

"Nah, I just had a bunch of stuff to do. I'm actually in the middle of something right now. Can you get to the point?" I asked her.

"I don't like this new you. I hardly talk to you anymore. The only time I see you is when I have to come over here without you knowing that I'm coming. It's been like this for a couple of weeks. I want to know what's going on, Sage," Leslie said.

"How did you know I was here? My car is in the garage, so how did you know?" I asked her.

"I just took a chance," she said.

"You sure you didn't follow me today?"

She'd been following me for the past two days. I knew, I just didn't care. Leslie had too much fucking time on her hands. She doesn't work, go to school, or even take an online class or two. She had time for all types of bullshit. This time, though, she's in the wrong place at the wrong time. Was I fucked up for the shit I was about to do and say? Possibly, but she came looking, so it was time for all her looking to pay off.

"Why are you not saying anything? You need to tell me what's going on with us. I'm not trying to lose you. We've been together for so long," she said as she walked over to me.

I backed up a few steps from her.

"We done," I told her.

"WHAT! You don't mean that," she said.

"Yes, I do. You've been following me for the past two days. Your dumb ass didn't even drive anybody else's car. How are you gonna follow a nigga in the car he bought? I swear you not all there sometimes. Just like I know you were parked up the street when I pulled up. Just like I know you only came up to the door to see if I had somebody in the house. You need some business, Leslie," I told her.

"If you knew I was following you, then why didn't you say that when I came to the door. I just wanted to see why you were giving me the cold shoulder all of a sudden," she said.

"I just didn't give a fuck. I wasn't doing shit anyway."

"Sage, do you have any smaller towels? All of these are way too big for my little body," Nailah said coming down the hallway.

She came down here with a fucking towel wrapped around her. Her hair was pulled up, and water was dripping everywhere.

I couldn't help but stare at her and bite my bottom lip. Nailah was fucking stacked. Yeah, I know she had a body and all, but damn. She was making the fucking towel look sexy as fuck right now.

"I'm sorry, I didn't know your girlfriend was here. I'll just make it work with this towel for the night," Nailah said then she turned and walked out of the room.

"This bitch. What is she doing here? What the fuck? Is this why you broke up with me?" Leslie asked.

"Man, get the fuck out!" I told her.

"How can you choose that bitch over me?" she asked.

I just laughed at Leslie and walked to the door. I opened the door for her and waited for her to walk her ass up out of there.

"You and that bitch are gonna be fucking sorry," Leslie said as she walked past me.

I popped her upside her head, which made her look back at me like I was crazy.

"Man, it was fly on ya," I told her.

Leslie rolled her eyes. She could do all the extra shit she wanted right now, but I hoped she took heed of the warning. I knew she was gonna be a problem, I just hoped I didn't have to take her ass out. I closed the door, turned the alarm on, and went to find Nailah.

"My bad about her coming over here. You don't have to worry about that again," I told her.

She was standing in the middle of the room with one of my t-shirts on. I had to remind myself to only look at her face and not the way she looked in my t-shirt. I think I got myself in trouble by bringing her to my home. She looked at her phone with an irritated expression before tossing it on the bed.

"Everything alright?" I asked.

"Yeah, Lox keeps texting me. I blocked his number, so I don't know whose number this is that keeps popping up. He's coming at me like I'm the one who messed up. I mean, he already had his backup plan, so what does he need me for? I just don't get men sometimes," she fussed.

I shrugged because I was taught that if you don't have anything good to say, you don't say nothing. Lox was probably the one who wants her dead just on the strength of him being a bitch.

"You're not gonna answer me?" she asked.

"You ain't ask me anything. I thought you were just venting or some shit," I told her.

I walked away from the room she was in. I didn't want to stay around her too much because the more I stayed around her, the more I wanted to fuck the shit out of her just to hear her scream out my name. I went to my room, took an extra-long shower, and took my ass to bed.

∞∞∞∞∞∞

"Get yo gay ass up. We got shit to do," Markos said.

"How the fuck you get in here?" I asked him.

"Doll Baby let me in. Yo, you need to take her to get her clothes or something because the way she looks in that t-shirt makes my ass wanna forget we used to eat mud pies together. Did you fuck her last night?" his stupid ass asked.

"Shut the fuck up and get out so I can get my shit together. Where the fuck we going anyway? Doll Baby is gonna have to come with us. I can't leave her alone, or the old heads will kill my ass," I told him.

"You think you slick, but yeah, alright. I'll tell her to get ready," Markos said.

He left, and I got up to get my shit together. I needed to get my mind right to be around Doll Baby all day. She was alright to chill with, but if I was around her all day, it might get hectic. Maybe she would just sit in the backseat and be quiet. I laughed at myself when I thought that. There was no way she was going to be quiet.

I got downstairs to the kitchen, and those two were in there talking and laughing. I watched for a few minutes and let them do their thing. There was no way he would sit there like this if it was Leslie. First of all, her ass wouldn't be in the kitchen cooking. My family didn't like to say her real name, so there was no sitting down to talk to her. Nailah or Doll Baby as we liked to call her behind her back was just a regular chick under all that damn beauty she had.

"You gonna come get something to eat, or are you gonna be a creep all day?" she asked me.

"How did you know I was standing here?" I asked.

"I just knew. Come eat. I need to go have a meeting with the lieutenants then I will go off the grid. I thought about still running everything, but I would need one contact person that I can trust, and I don't know them like that," she said.

It was good that she was thinking about business with her life on the line, but she wasn't running shit 'til we figured out what was going on.

"Get Montay to do it. He doesn't owe any allegiance to those niggas, so he'll be more critical of them. He also doesn't play when it comes to you. You will most likely have to replace a few of 'em knowing him," Markos said.

"You sure he would do it for me?" she asked.

"You family, but for real, Montay loves you. But you're Sage's pop wife, so he's not gonna push up on you. It's all love," Markos said.

I knew he was just waiting to say that. She looked all confused, which made him start laughing. I swear this nigga got on my damn nerves sometimes. I had forgotten all about that shit, but leave it up to his ass to bring some shit like that up.

"Are y'all gonna tell me what it is? I'm saying, do I have to get a pop divorce or something?" she asked with a smile on her face.

"We used to get those pop ring suckers all the time. One day we were all playing, and this girl from down the street came over. Everybody had a pop ring but her. She was asking everybody for one. When she got to Sage to ask, he told her hell nah. You came up and told him that he could have yours. Yours was already open, and you had already licked it and everything. His wasn't open yet. Of course, we were some extra ass kids back then. He gave his to the girl, and you gave him yours. When he licked it after you, we started clowning him and shit. I mean, think about it, you had already licked the damn thing. In our eyes, that was just like kissing. We started calling you his pop wife after that," Markos explained.

"It's fucked up that I don't remember all that shit like y'all do. I remember coming over to play with y'all and stuff. I remembered some stuff when Sage showed me the picture," she said.

"I texted Montay to meet us at your spot for the meeting," I told her.

"Yes sir, my dear sweet pop husband," she said and laughed.

"You talk too fucking much," I told Markos.

"Hey, I'm just trying to keep the divorce rate down," Markos said with a laugh.

I shook my head at his dumb ass. This was going to be a long ass day.

16 – MONTAY

I was a street nigga since the age of ten. I caught my first body when I was seventeen. I was close to Sage and Markos because we were always around each other. I respected the fact that they never got into the family business, but I also knew that they were groomed to take over if anything happens to the old heads. We were all put here on earth for a purpose. I accepted the fact that mine was to be the nigga I am today.

I just got the text from Sage saying we had to meet up. I made my way over there before I got down to the business that I needed to handle. I didn't know the address that he sent me. I put it in my GPS, and I pulled up to it within ten minutes. Sage, Markos, and Nailah pulled up before I could get out of the car. We all followed her so she could open the door.

"Ya place is dope as fuck," I said.

Nailah laughed at me as we all sat down.

"I have a proposition for you," Nailah said.

"I ain't having a threesome with you and Sage. He's my cousin, and that's some nasty shit," I told them.

I was dead ass right now. They wanna laugh at me, but I didn't give a fuck. That shit was nasty.

"I know your mama dropped your ass when you were born for sure now," Sage said.

"I want you to be the face of my shit. You wouldn't really have too much to do. Making drops and making sure they not out here wilding out is the most you would have to do," she told me.

"Okay," I said.

"Montay, that was quick. I thought you were going to need time to think about it. You can get back to me in a couple of days," she said.

"I just told you I would do it. What the hell is the problem?" I asked her.

"You answered a little quick on this. I know you already doing stuff for your family," Nailah said.

"What you saying? Your ass is family too. I just said yeah, so say thank you and shut the fuck up," I told her.

I turned and left them in the house. I had to get my shit in order before taking the head of Nailah's shit. It's a lot of fucking work running shit in these streets. I don't see how the OG's loved doing this shit day in and day out. I'm not complaining, but damn. I'm not gonna do this shit all my fucking life. I was gonna retire then find me a no surgery having bitch to fuck on a boat. Y'all laugh all you want, but finding a chick who hasn't gone under the knife was rare. Even bitches in the hood were spending income tax checks to get some work done.

I pulled up to one of the house we had in the hood. I went from zero to hundred real fucking quick. These young motherfuckers don't believe shit you tell them. I tell them all the time don't be hanging all outside and shit.

Everyone who worked for us didn't have any fucking social media accounts either. If you're doing illegal shit, there is no need for the extra bullshit social media brought with it. I know you say, well how the hell do you know what they have? Well, all our workers' phones have a chip in them. We can see every fucking thing they do on them damn things. They all young, so the most they did was sext with some thot and talk shit about us. I didn't mind them talking that shit, though. When they start acting out and shit, that's when shit gets crazy.

I hopped out of the car and walked up on the first nigga I saw. I started hitting that nigga like he got my little sister pregnant.

"I told you young niggas not to have a bunch of young thots hanging around out here!" I yelled.

He was laying on the ground not moving. I knew he wasn't dead because I saw his chest moving up and down. My phone rang, so I held back what I was gonna say to answer the call.

"Hello," I answered calmly.

"I keep telling your hot-headed ass you can't keep fucking up these young wolves like that out in public. You wanna kick their asses then you take that shit to the basement. Think before you act, nigga. Don't worry about how I knew because I know every fucking thing. You need to come and see me after you pick that young wolf up. Don't do shit else, just come straight here. Don't even call Keisha's ass," my dad said before ending the call.

I helped the little nigga up. He looked like he was scared for his life. I don't know why my pops called these niggas wolves. They were more like poodle puppies or some punk ass dog like that. Leave it up to my dad to still be watching me even though I've been doing this for damn near five years now. I walked my ass to the car to go find out what Michael Young wanted with me. I knew there had to be something else besides me fucking up the youngin'.

"Dad, what you need?" I asked as I closed his front door.

"I need you to get a fucking stress ball or something. Stop beating on them youngins like that. You must need to fuck or something. It's ridiculous that you're beating on them like you're their father or something. If they not listening, let them go, plain and simple. Your ass trying to stay in shape by fucking them boys up all the time," he told me.

I looked at him and laughed. My father was the baby brother, but they all looked like triplets. If they never told you, there was no way you could tell what the order of their ages are. Sage's pops, Maurice, was the oldest, then came Marko's pops, whose name is Mark, then my dad Michael. They were all retired or, so they said. They were very much in the know of what was going on in the streets.

"I know about you accepting to be the face of Khan's operation. Are you sure that is a step you're willing to make?" he asked.

"Yeah, I can do it. I mean, if Lox's dumb ass can do it, I know I can. It doesn't take a rocket scientist. I'm not merging cells or no shit like that, so I'm good. Didn't y'all groom me for this shit? It doesn't matter who I do it for. I'm not gonna be doing it long either, so we good," I told him.

"There are other factors in this that y'all don't know about," he told me.

"Well, make that shit known. Y'all keep all this shit on the hush, leaving us out here blind."

They act like we were the ones who were trying to do some foul shit. They needed to let us in on what's going on instead of playing these games.

"Y'all not blind. You just not looking hard enough. Sometimes you gotta think outside of the box," Dad told me.

I shook my head and went to wash my hands. I knew he wasn't gonna give me any more info, so there was no need to ask. They had been like this even when we were in school. If we asked them something, they would rephrase it, and we would end up answering our own question. Those Young brothers were some smart motherfuckers. They just made you work for answers and shit.

"Dad, I'm 'bout to be out. I'll think about what you said. Just so you know, I'm gonna put somebody on Lox too just in case he wants to jump stupid," I told him.

"Good move," I heard him say before I closed the door.

I knew it was a good move, that's why I made the motherfucker.

17 - LOX

A few weeks had passed since I last talked to Nailah. I'd been calling her and shit, trying to get her to talk to me. DeJa, on the other hand, is the one I've been trying to get away from. I was staying at a hotel at first, but she hunted me down. I was staying with her because I needed to get my shit together. I'd been spending money on these birds because I never thought Nailah would put my ass out in real life. She had always been the one constant since we first got together. DeJa couldn't take care of me like Nailah could.

DeJa was just a chick that I had history with. She always thought that we belonged together. I only thought that she was some convenient pussy. I know she loves me and all that, but that's not my problem. For now, I was gonna use that shit to my advantage. I'm pissed that she went to Nailah with the shit she told her, but I should have expected it.

For the moment, I was staying with her ass in the hood. I'm not used to this bullshit. She doesn't do a damn thing that a woman should. No cleaning, cooking, I even got more pussy and head from her before I had to stay with her. This shit had me stressed because I needed to get a fucking come up quick.

"You need to do something else besides lounging around

here. I mean, you supposed to be the man, but you don't have a backup plan? You can't expect shit to come to you by sitting on my fucking couch, Lox," DeJa complained in my ear.

"You the reason I'm on your couch in the first place. I should beat your ass every time I think about this shit. You knew what my plans were, but you still sashayed your ass to her house. I'll get off this fucking couch whenever I fucking feel like it," I told her.

"You still love her more than you love me, but I'm the one still with your dog ass," DeJa said.

"You knew that I was with Nailah from the beginning. I never lied to you about my relationship with her. It's always been about her since me and her got together. You wanna act like you mad because I'm out here fucking other bitches. The real reason you mad is that you will never be Nailah. At the end of the day, you only gonna be some project bitch with an insurance plan on her cell phone and not her life," I told her.

"Don't think you gonna stay here with me and talk to me like this. I'm helping you out with your hustling backward ass. Who the fuck plans a takeover but doesn't have no money in the bank? You should even have a house somewhere by now. Not you, though, you too busy out here fucking all these hoes instead of working on your fucking plan in the first place. She done put word out that you not to be fucked with in these streets. Nobody's gonna put you on because you don't have a loyal bone in your body. You can put this shit on me all you want. I'm the one who knocked on her door, but your ass is on my couch because you will never be a boss. You always gonna be low on the totem pole with your dumb ass," DeJa said.

"Get the fuck on, DeJa. You gonna make me fuck you up," I told her.

She laughed in my face. The look on her face showed no love and all disgust.

"I'm gonna need you to leave because I have somebody coming over," DeJa said.

It was my turn to laugh because I know she didn't think that shit was gonna go down with me there. I ignored her as best I could, but her mouth kept going.

"You don't have the coin that you used to kick this way, so I need better options. Don't act like you didn't know what the deal was. I love you, but I love the coin way more. You're messing up my flow without adding to my pockets. I have shit to do," she said.

"DeJa, don't make me kill you in here. You better go meet that nigga somewhere else. Make sure you bring me back a pack of cigarillos and some weed," I told her.

"Nigga, fuck you and your broke ass, I got bills to pay."

"Let me find out you out here fucking to pay your twenty-five-dollar rent. Your utilities are included, so you only have one fucking bill to pay," I told her.

She out here fucking for chump change and weed. I should pimp her ass out until I get on my feet. That's exactly what I'm gonna do. She got me in this shit, so she was gonna get me out of it. I was gonna wait 'til she came in tonight to let her know about her new job. I bet the next time she wanna be a nigga's side bitch she'll know her fucking place.

"I hope you don't think I'm gonna be leaving every time I need to entertain my company. You need to go ahead with your plan. You just gonna have to take over from the outside instead of the inside. She couldn't have changed that much. I don't care what you do, but you not gonna keep cramping my style. I need my coin no matter where it comes from," DeJa said.

I laughed at her as she went out the door. She was in for a rude awakening when she walked her ass in tonight. I was gonna lay that pimp smackdown on her ass. In the meantime, I had a few hours to kill, so I needed to walk around the hood and find out what Nailah was up to.

I hopped in the shower, put my clothes on, and went out the door. My first stop was gonna be the main house. I still had a couple of dudes that would give me the info I needed. These bitches were gonna be begging me to keep them alive before all of this was over.

∞∞∞∞∞∞∞∞

I had walked by the main house and two other houses I knew Nailah had, but they were all shut down. I was calling my boys, but no one was answering the phone. I got a bad feeling because it had to be something big going on for not one of them niggas to answer the phone. I hadn't seen them while I was walking around either, so something major had to be up.

I stopped by the corner store to get a soda and a slice of pizza. I had to sit down and think to figure out how the hell I could still take over Nailah's shit. I wanted to knock her off her fucking queens shit she was on. Her dad's name and clout wasn't gonna be what saved her. I looked up and saw one of my boys' old ladies walking into the corner store. She saw me, and she rushed over looking like she wanted to cry.

"I know you killed him. He told me that he had a meeting to go to, and I haven't seen him since. How is it that my man is dead, and you in here eating pizza like you're on *Do the Right Thing*?" she fussed.

"Whoa, baby girl, you need to calm down. I didn't do shit to ya boy. I haven't been running shit for a while. The last time I saw him, he was alive, and I left his ass that way. Don't be going around blaming me for shit and not have any proof. I see you emotional, so I'mma let that shit slide for now. I'll find out what happened, though, and let you know," I told her.

She looked me up and down with tears falling down her cheeks. Then she slapped the shit out of me.

"I don't need you to walk away and make up a lie. I know the motto out here. *No body, no case*, that's how it goes, right? I can feel it that he's dead. I just pray that you catch the same fate that he did. Shit didn't start going left until he started hanging around you more. You a fucking plague out here. I hope you suffer before you get dealt the same fate, motherfucker," she told me.

If I had been the one to kill her man, I might have felt bad. I didn't kill the nigga, so I wasn't pressed about what she was talking about. I just hoped she wasn't out here telling people I killed him. Then, I would have to kill her. She'll find that nigga then, that's for damn sure. I tried to call Nailah again. My call went straight to voicemail. I knew she blocked my ass, but that wasn't gonna be enough to get rid of me. I was gonna have to go find her ass. I finished my food and headed out to my mom's house so I could use her car. I couldn't walk to the other side of town.

I got to my mom's house, and there was an extra car in the driveway. I'd never seen the car before, but it was nice as fuck. I guess moms was trying to get her groove back. I knew she was gonna go off as soon as I got in the house because she had to know about the break up by now. I walked in, not expecting to see her at the table deep in a conversation with Nailah's dad.

"Ma, what's going on?" I asked, not caring about interrupting their conversation.

"Hello to you too, Luther," she said.

She knew I hated that fucking name. I could tell by her tone that they had to have been talking about me.

"Why is Nailah's dad here?" I asked.

"He came to see if I could talk some sense into you. I never thought I raised a stalker or a gigolo. You had a good woman, but you couldn't keep your dick in your pants. I'm so disappointed in you," she said.

"Hold up. What goes on with me and her doesn't have shit to do with either of y'all," I told her.

"You need to watch your mouth," Nailah's pops said.

"That's my damn momma. You might put fear in the hearts of the niggas out here in the streets, but I'm not them. You can get the fuck out. Fuck you and your hoe of a daughter," I told him.

"That's your problem. You always want to sound like you're a man. You don't know the first thing about being a man. It's not about how loud you can be, how much money you claim to have, or how many females you fuck. A man is built on honor, loyalty, and a sense of pride. You have to give respect to get it. Be careful out here, it would be a shame if I have to hold your mother up through your funeral services," Nailah's pops said.

"You threatening me? You, old motherfucker," I said as I walked up in his face. I don't know what Nailah had told him, but I will fuck his old ass up.

"Son, you need to calm down and think about your actions. You also can stay away from Nailah. Don't call or try to see her. If you do, then I will have to show your young ass that my street days are not over. I'm giving you a chance to live," he told me.

"I'll keep on living. What the fuck can your old ass do to me?" I asked him.

"LUTHER!" my mom yelled.

"Ma, you can stop with all that hollering. He ain't never liked me. I guess he finally got to Nailah and made her leave me. I hope you enjoy your little time. She'll take me back as soon as I talk to her. She been ducking me, but I'll catch up to her sooner or later. She can't avoid me forever," I told him.

"She's not avoiding you. She's being protected by someone who loves her and wants nothing but the best for my baby girl. You are the last thing on her mind," he told me.

I knew he was just talking to get me upset. I was pissed, but he wouldn't know it. His old ass always acting like he has all the answers. I nodded my head at him. I wasn't going to keep going back and forth with him. He might be her dad, but she belonged to me.

Chapter Eighteen

18 – LESLIE

The only reason I hadn't gone off the deep end is that I had two secret accounts that Sage didn't know about. Being out on the street could never be an option for me. I will never be a bitch that anyone could say 'damn, she used to have it all.' I was on top, and that's where I planned to stat. I just had to find a way to make Sage take me back. He was my fucking meal ticket until that damn bitch came along. She fucked up my life, so it was my turn to fuck up hers.

I had to find a way to get her away from Sage. If she wasn't in the picture, he would need me just like he always has. Sage could front all he wanted to, but if he didn't love me, he wouldn't have kept me around for so long. He fussed and complained about how I needed to make my own mark in the world, but he still stayed. Maybe if I started going to school, I would show him that I was more than he thought I was. I just needed to get the money to go to school. I couldn't take out a loan or anything trivial like that. The thought of going to school alone made my skin crawl.

I decided to get my ass up and try to go talk some sense into Sage. I knew he was at his office right now. That's one thing I loved about Sage. He was always a man willing to work no matter what was going on in his personal life. I made sure I had on the tightest pencil skirt that I could wear and still sit down without looking crazy. My shirt was open enough to make any man want to see more. I was pulling out all the stops today. Hopefully, this would work. If not, then I would have to resort to less ladylike tactics. I gave myself a look before heading out the door to go get my man back.

I waltzed into Sage's office with my head held high. I saw his old bitty of a secretary at the front desk. I knew she was surprised to see me.

"I need to see Sage, can you page him to let him know that I'm coming up?" I told her.

"He's not here. Mr. Young is on vacation, and he's not coming back for another two weeks," she said.

"Vacation? He never goes on vacation. He's a workaholic. I know he's in there," I told her.

I walked around her desk heading to his office door. I could hear her coming behind me. I was almost at the door when I heard Markos' voice.

"The fuck are you doing here?" Markos asked.

"I'm here to see your cousin. Call him and let him know that I'm here," I told him.

"No," he simply answered.

"What do you mean no? I need to see him," I told him.

"How many definitions do you think the word no has? He's not here. Even if he was, he wouldn't want to see you. Leave, Leslie," Markos told me.

"Sage loves me despite all of you acting like I'm not good enough for him. He always was there for me. That type of love doesn't happen overnight. It damn sure doesn't go away overnight," I told him.

He chuckled at me like I was comical to him. This motherfucker has always been a pain in my ass. The feeling was mutual.

"Like I said, he's not here. He's not coming back today or the next day. He's somewhere enjoying himself for a change with some company that doesn't give him a fucking headache or drive him deeper into debt. Get your ass up and get the fuck on before I throw your ass out," Markos told me.

I knew that was something he wanted to do, but I wouldn't give him the satisfaction of putting his hands on me.

"You wish you could touch me. I know I'm better than any hood rat ass bitch that you stick your little dick in," I told him.

He grabbed my hand and put it on his dick. He made me massage his dick while he stood there with that disgusting smirk on his face.

"My dick is never small, bitch. When you speak on my shit, put some respect on it. I bet your garbage ass pussy wet now, ain't it. Go 'head and play with your pussy in the parking lot," he told me.

I can't believe he did that. I stood there with my mouth open and looking at my hand from the shock.

"My dick so big it has you contemplating life decisions, don't it?" he asked me.

"You're a disgusting mother fucker," I told him.

"I can put some toothpaste on my dick before I shove it in your mouth. You need to clean your mouth out. It's not cute to be a lady with a dirty mouth," he said.

I rolled my eyes and walked out of the office. I made sure to hit him with my twenty-four inches.

"You need to stop throwing other people's shit around like that. That shit's rude as hell. I should smack the fuck outta you. I'll save that shit for my new cousin-in-law," he said.

"I know he didn't marry that bitch already. I've been with him for all these years and he up and marries her of all people?" I said, turning around.

"It ain't about the years you put in. Sage ain't a fucking job, what the hell you on? Yeah, he married her. It doesn't take some niggas years to know if you the one or not. Besides, I bet his dick got hard every time he saw you leave the house. He was praying and wishing you get sideswiped by a fucking eighteen-wheeler carrying a bunch of bumblebees so they can sting the fuck outta you," he said laughing.

I couldn't hold back the tears. I was sobbing in front of Markos, and he was standing there unbothered. Sage's secretary ran to get me some tissues as I sat on the bench in the hallway.

"Nah, don't get comfortable. You need to go outside to cry and snot in whatever car you came here in. We ain't got time for all that." He grabbed me by the arm and forced me out of the building.

I gathered myself the best that I could and went to the car. If he was married, there was no way I was going to get him back. I cried in the car for twenty minutes. When I finally got myself together, I noticed the mark on my arm that Markos left. I smiled, made a phone call, and pulled off. Game on, mother fucker. I'll see who's laughing by the end of the day.

19 – SAGE

Bringing Nailah to Aruba was the best thing I could have done. We both needed a break from our realities. Montay was busy putting her street shit back in order, and Markos was handling things at the office for me. I was enjoying the weather and seeing Nailah in her bathing suits every day. I had to remind myself that we were not here for us to get close; we both were supposed to be relaxing. I couldn't focus on relaxing because every time I closed my eyes, I saw Nailah in a two-piece with her hair all wet. Skin glistening with sprinkles of water under the sunlight. The shit was turning into torture.

"Sage!" Nailah called to me.

"What's up?" I answered.

"I think we should go out tonight. We need to see what the club scene is like on the island. It'll be fun, don't you think so?" she asked.

"Yup, real fun," I replied unenthusiastically.

"Don't be like that. It'll be fun. Just us having fun. That's what we're here for, right? To have fun. Let our hair down, so to speak," she said smiling.

"Did you get your number changed?" I asked her.

"I did. I also changed cell phone companies. My dad said he

was gonna go talk to his mom. I don't know why though," she said.

"We not here to talk about that. I just wanted to make sure that was done before we got back home. I never want you to be caught out here half stepping. I'll protect you with my life if I have to. You need to remember that. All of us will," I told her seriously.

"I know, and the same goes for me. I guess I need to get ready for tonight. I just might find my mandingo while were out tonight," she said.

"No fucking comment on that shit," I told her.

She laughed like I was joking around. I wish some nigga would try to lay her down tonight. This wasn't a dick hunting trip for her.

I heard the door close, letting me know that she left. I knew I was gonna have weed on deck and already rolled fucking with Nailah tonight. This was gonna be some shit that I had to be high and tipsy for at least. I was having a hard enough time not tripping and having my dick fall in her pussy as it is. I pray that the lord of lawyers with thug tendencies lays his mercy on me tonight because I was damn sure gonna need it.

∞∞∞∞∞∞∞∞

I knocked on the door that connected Nailah's room to mine. I felt like an eighth grader going to his first co-ed dance. I chose to go casual tonight. We were on the island, so I had on some off-white linen pants with a matching shirt. I finished the outfit off with my platinum Rolex and ring. I had on some uncle sandals, but they were appropriate for the night. I prayed that the lord didn't make me suffer too bad tonight.

She opened the door, and I knew I was in big ass trouble.

"Shit," I said before I could stop myself.

I looked her up and down, instantly regretting that I agreed to go out with her tonight. She had on an off-white dress. I know that sounds simple, but this shit was gonna make me crazy all night. It looked like it was just one piece of cloth that she put her arms in. The top of the dress barely covered her chest. There was a big ass dip in the front that she had a sparkling chain dangling from her neck to occupy the open space. I don't know why the fuck she thought that was a good idea. It was only gonna make niggas look at her damn chest. There was a split, I guess on the right side, and her right leg was decorated with one of those temporary Henna tattoos. I'm talking about her whole fucking leg was decorated. She didn't have shoes on because the club was on the beach, but she had on them damn foot chains on both feet.

This is not gonna fucking work.

I ran my hand across my waves, which made her laugh. I guess she felt like this torture she was putting me under was funny. I shook my head and walked away from her. I couldn't believe she was wearing that shit tonight. I needed to get a bottle quick as fuck.

We got to the club, and the vibe was chill for the most part. I was too busy making sure there wasn't an island nigga waiting to try Nailah. I tried to stay close to her, but not so close that she thought I was blocking. Yeah, I was blocking, but I didn't need that argument right now.

The entire club was on the beach. I'm talking tables on the beach with a hole in the middle where a fire was burning. The dance floor was marked by a big ass square made of outside lights that we use in America to line out driveways. The moon looked like it was sitting on top of the water. This shit was hot on some real shit. This was some movie type of atmosphere. The island music playing in the background topped everything off.

"It's so beautiful here. Thank you for kidnapping me and making me come. I needed this more than I knew. I don't wanna go home now," she said.

"You don't have to if you don't want to. I own the resort

we're staying in. Just let me know when you're ready. We're on your time," I told her.

"WHAT! You never told me that. We might stay the rest of the month then," she said.

"It's whatever you want. It's all about you, Doll Baby," I told her.

I hardly ever called her that. In my mind, Nailah and Doll Baby were two different people. Nailah was just a business associate. She was the more cutthroat of the two. She didn't play when it came to business. A smile was something you never saw when you were dealing with Nailah. Now, Doll Baby, she was a sweetheart who didn't mind being vulnerable. She was so goofy that she would laugh at something for an hour that wasn't even funny to me. She didn't mind asking questions or trying new things, which is why I called her Doll Baby because Nailah would come out there with a sexy ass pantsuit on, heels and all. The only skin Nailah showed was her face, neck, hands, maybe a few toes, but that was it.

"You don't say Doll Baby like everyone else. It sounds like there's genuine care and love behind it. It makes me feel weird," she told me.

"I don't know what you're talking 'bout. Let me find out you already drunk, and we just got here." I laughed as I lied to her.

I prayed that she moved on and didn't keep pressing the issue. She tilted her head to the side, looking like she was planning another question in her head. When she bit her lip, my heart dropped to my pants.

"Come dance with me?" she asked.

"You know I don't dance. I guess I can for you just this once. If you tell anybody, I'll kill ya," I said with a laugh.

She grabbed me by the hand and led the way to the designated spot for dancing. I couldn't call it a dancefloor because there was no floor. Anyway, I watched her ass the whole way there. I wonder if she had on thongs or nothing at all. The way her cheeks were jiggling, it had to be one of the two. It had to be jelly because jam don't shake like that.

"Don't punk out on me and leave me on the dancefloor by myself," she said jokingly.

"I would never leave you anywhere," I said seriously, but with a smile.

We danced to about three fast songs, then some smooth, slow Jamaican song came on. I didn't even know they made slow songs. Most of the time them joints be all fast and shit. This one sounded good as hell though. It was some chick singing. All I could tell you was that she was singing about some man. Now what that nigga did to make her sad, I have no idea, but I was happy as hell he did the shit.

Nailah put her head against my chest. I was so much taller than her that I just placed my chin on the top of her head. I wasn't thinking about her smooshing my beard or making it smell like that fruity shit she puts in her hair. I was just enjoying this moment. This was our moment, our memory. I hoped she felt as comfortable in my arms as I did with her in mine. My mind was telling me to let her go, but my heart and soul were screaming for me to hold her tighter. I did just that, and I held on to her like I would never let her go.

"I remember when we were in love like that. That's right, young man, you better hold on to her tight. Love like this only comes once in a lifetime. Take it from a man who almost lost the love of his life. You two look like you'll make some beautiful babies. Keep her close to you, young man," this older black man said to us.

The whole time I was holding her, I didn't even pay it any mind that we weren't the only people dancing. In my mind, we were the only ones there. I need to get it together. This was not the point of the trip.

"I've never made love before," she told me softly.

"Huh? What did you say?" I asked.

"All these years with Lox, and maybe two other guys who

don't even need to be mentioned. I have never been made love to. I haven't experienced true lovemaking. You know the love-making that you see in movies, or you read about in books. The kind of love that touches your soul instead of the back of your inner walls," she said.

"You will one day," I told her, not wanting to go there with her.

"Tonight," she said.

"Tonight, what?" I asked.

"I want you to make love to me tonight," she said.

This whole time we had been dancing in a repetitive sway. When she said that, I stopped. I looked at her to see if I could tell if she was drunk, playing, or what. I saw her looking at me and wanting me to agree with her. She wanted me to say yes to her. I took her by the hand and led her away from the other people.

"You want me to stick my dick in your pussy, Doll Baby?" I asked her.

She placed her hands on the sides of my face, and our lips met halfway. So soft, but firm enough to know that she was serious about what she was asking me to do. I stopped the kiss because I didn't want to get all wrapped up in her right now. Who the fuck am I kidding? I was already wrapped up in Nailah Khan aka Doll Baby and everything about her. I picked her up, and she wrapped her legs around me. I didn't care that we were on a beach that was serving as a club right now.

"Yes, Sage. I understand if you don't want to. Just tell me if you don't. I won't ask you about it anymore, I promise," she babbled.

I scooped her up bridal style, and we headed to the room. I hoped she ready for all the pressure I had built up in me. It's been a few weeks since me and Leslie did anything. The first thing I had to do was see if she had on thongs or nothing. I moved the little bit of fabric that the dress was made of to be greeted with the most beautiful vagina I'd ever seen. She had her completely bald. I looked for evidence of shaving bumps, but it was smooth as a baby's ass.

I bit the pussy. Yes, I bit it like it was a fucking apple, peach, or whatever piece of fruit there was that you bite. I felt her hands on my waves then I placed little kisses all over her. I parted her lips with my tongue and put her legs over my shoulder one by one. I felt the elevator start to move, but I wasn't stopping. She was moaning and squeezing my head, which only made me go harder.

I rubbed on her ass cheeks as she squirmed around. I heard the elevator doors open, and I looked over my shoulder with the essence of her coating my beard. An older couple stood there. The lady had her hand over her mouth while her husband was smiling his ass off.

"This one is out of order. Catch the next one," I said.

I didn't wait for them to respond or the doors to close before I went back to my late-night snack.

"Sage, baby stop. We on the elevator," she moaned.

"Shut the hell up. I own this bitch," I said then I smacked her ass.

She went back to moaning, but she never told me to stop again. I waited for her to cum twice while we were on the elevator before I tossed her over my shoulder. As I carried her to my room, I bit and smacked her ass. I opened the door and kicked it shut once I walked in.

Chapter Twenty

20 – NAILAH

"*A*in't no need to get scared now," Sage said.

He was standing over me with his overly large dick in his hand. I was tipsy when I asked him to make love to me and while he was eating me out on the elevator. Once he pulled his third leg out, I sobered up really quick.

"Can we talk about this?" I asked as I scooted off the bed.

"Let me find out that nigga had a baby dick. You're fucking with a real nigga now, Doll Baby," he said as he walked toward me.

My back hit the wall. *Damn, I thought this room was bigger.*

"I told you I would make love to you, right? I'm a man of my word. Stop running," he said.

"I don't need all types of surgeries and medical bills behind one night," I told him seriously.

"I haven't had any complaints before. Stop fucking playing. I'll go slow the first round," he said with a smile.

"FIRST ROUND!" I yelled.

"You can handle it."

Sage had me in the corner trapped. He kissed me on the neck. I fell into the trap and closed my eyes while throwing my head back. The next thing I knew, I was being picked up with my legs wrapped around his waist. He laid me down on the bed, and before I could think about what was going to happen, he was inside me. I could feel my insides being stretched like a rubber band.

"Bite my shoulder if you have to, baby," he whispered.

I felt him stop moving. I could hear him mumbling to himself, but I couldn't make out what he was saying or trying to say. Slowly, he started moving in and out of me. He moved with slow, deliberate motions. Once it got more comfortable with him inside me, he started kissing on my breasts and licking a nipple here and there. I was trying not to get lost in the feeling he was giving me.

This was something foreign to me. When Lox and I would have sex, it was always just sex. It was nothing like this. This was something different, it was so much more than I asked for.

Sage was learning my body. It was like he was trying to see what drove me crazier. This man was rocking my world. I felt tingles from my toes to the top of my ears. I wasn't seeing stars or no shit like that, but this shit was on another level.

He sped up his strokes just a little bit. Then he started making all kinds of crazy grunting noises. He was biting his bottom lip while little beads of sweat dripped off him. My eyes started to roll in the back of my head. I started screaming like Jason Voorhees from *Friday The Thirteenth* was behind me. This man was killing my pussy and all the expectations I had of him.

"Sage, I'm about to cum again," I called out to him.

"Fuck you telling me for? Do that shit," he grunted back as he looked me in the eyes.

We came together while staring into each other's eyes. I felt something pass between us in that moment. It felt like we were connected more than sexually or physically. We made love all over his room, eventually falling asleep naked holding each other.

The next morning, I woke up to an empty bed. I knew we were in his room, so I had no clue where he could've gone. I got up and went to my room to take a shower then maybe get some breakfast. I was in the shower fighting the flashbacks of last-night from invading my mind. I don't know what it was about Sage, but I'd never felt like that after a night of sex with Lox. I felt like I was missing something. I know I wasn't missing anything physically, but I felt incomplete and out of place.

Tears ran down my face. I knew that I was in trouble. How was I going to live with this man? This was supposed to be a one-time thing, but my pussy was getting wet just thinking about him and his touch. We were connected, like in sync with each other connected. I was in another world trying to think of ways to avoid Sage when the shower curtain was pulled back.

There he was standing there with no shirt on, just a pair of gray basketball shorts. My eyes went automatically to the front of his shorts. I saw it getting harder in a matter of seconds. I caught myself licking my lips until he put his hand in front of his dick and tossed a towel at me.

"Come on, we gotta talk," he said with a stone face.

He walked out before I could respond. I got nervous suddenly, but I dried off then wrapped myself in the towel before going in the room where he was. I walked in slowly.

"Why you look like you 'bout to get a beating?" he asked, laughing at me.

He handed me a bag of food.

"Thank you," I told him.

"How do you feel? I'm saying, are you sore or anything?" he asked.

"No, I'm fine," I lied.

He looked like he was mad I said that I was fine.

"I don't want us to change," he said.

"I know. I don't either. I asked for it, and I admit that it was way more than I ever thought it would be," I told him honestly.

"So, you felt that shit too? That shit was crazy. I'm not a soft ass nigga, but I swear the gates of heaven opened up last night," he said with a smile. When I didn't respond, he started talking again. "Doll Baby, I'm not gonna lie, this shit's gonna be awkward as fuck. I don't regret nothing we did last night. But, still, we both understand that this doesn't mean that we're a couple or no shit like that. We just helped each other out while we were out here," he said.

I was shocked that he was so cool about everything. He just said that the gates of heaven opened up, but then we were just helping each other out in the next breath. Helping each other out like he helped me change a fucking flat tire. I guess I read more into things than he did. I agree that this was a line that we had crossed, but I can cross back over that bitch like nothing happened. I hope I can, anyway.

"Do you get what I'm trying to say?" he asked.

I nodded my head up and down. I hoped that my broken soul didn't show on my face. I bounced up from where I was sitting and looked through the drawers to find my clothes for the day. I really needed to do something with myself before I broke down crying or cussing at Sage. I don't know what I was expecting to feel, but this heartbreak wasn't it.

"Yeah, I get what you're saying. I need to find something to do. We only have a few days left," I told him.

"Nailah, I'm not trying to say that we not..." he tried to explain.

"Sage! I get it. Now, can you leave so I can find something to wear? We still have an island to enjoy," I said with a smile.

He looked at me like he wanted to still explain, but I put my hand up to stop him before he started again. He shook his head and left out of the room. Once I was sure he was gone, I sat on the corner of the bed and cried until I couldn't anymore. I should have known that this was going to end badly. Now I had to be around him and act like last night didn't change my life. Lord be with me.

∞∞∞∞∞∞

The last few days on the island were as beautiful as the others, but it was intensely uncomfortable. We still hung out doing things like swimming with the dolphins, riding horses on the beach, and driving ATVs. The laughter was still there, but there was also tension in the air. How could we feel so deeply for each other yet feel like we don't know each other at the same time?

Now, we were on the plane heading back to the states. I was on one side of the plane, and he was on the other. We were both into our phones, obviously avoiding each other. I didn't know what Sage was doing, but I was looking for a condo to move into as soon as possible. Just the thought of living in the same house with him was giving me a headache.

I also had been in contact with Montay. He agreed that being the head of the organization now meant that it would be better for him to meet with Sage and Markos regarding the business deal that we had with them. I was sure he wanted to ask why I asked him to step in for me. He never asked, so I never explained. I had no intention of telling him or Markos about the plan to move out on my own. I knew that they would be all too happy to tell Sage. I was looking into getting my own security detail because Lox was still running around being the bitter bitch ass nigga that he was. I knew that when I did move, it was gonna be some shit. I could handle it though, I guess.

21 – BALTIMORE

I must admit that even though I fought Markos on everything he wanted to do for me, I appreciated him nonetheless. I knew my neighbors thought that I was crazy the way I cussed him out when he brought me my new 2017 BMW X5 truck. We argued for almost an hour about how that was not a 'just to get around' vehicle. He had the nerve to tell me that he didn't spend his money on nothing other than a BMW or Mercedes. The way he saw it was that he bought the basic model, so it was a beginner's vehicle.

Everything was in my name so I wouldn't feel like I was at his mercy. He even told me that I could cook for him every Sunday for the next three years to pay the truck off. He wasn't taking any money, though.

I had gotten used to him coming over and acting like the asshole big brother that I never had. The thing that blew my mind was when I found out he went to my boss to let him know that I was getting a promotion. Yup, you read that right. Markos Young went to my boss at the restaurant to tell him that I was getting a raise. I don't know what he did or said to my manager, but I was now the assistant manager at the restaurant. I didn't work any late hours, and my schedule always allowed for me to be off on Sundays, of course. I was pretty sure he had someone watching me although he always denied it.

I was in the kitchen fixing Markos his weekly Sunday dinner. I expected him to call like he did every Sunday morning asking if I needed anything for dinner. He was having food delivered from the grocery store just like he promised, but he still checked to see if I needed anything else. I hadn't heard from him today, which meant he had partied late last night. I never asked details of his personal life, but I did wonder from time to time.

I was putting the lasagna in the oven when there was a knock on the door. I opened the door to find Montay standing on my porch with a phone in his hand. He gave me a head nod and handed me the phone.

"Hello," I answered.

"Baltimore, I need a favor," Markos said.

"Where are you? Are you okay?" I asked.

"I need you to follow Montay to the precinct, so when he bails me out, I can come straight to your house," he said.

"Okay, let me turn the food off," I told him.

I handed Montay the phone back, turned the oven off, and closed up the house. When I came outside, Montay was looking at me and smiling. He always did that when I was around. He never said much to me, though. I needed to ask Markos what was up with him. First, I needed to know why he was in jail in the first place.

I sat in the car while Montay went in the building. There was no need for me to be inside. I was only there for transportation purposes. I was playing some dumb ass bubble popping game on my phone when Markos tapped on the window. I popped the lock to let the criminal in.

"What's up, convict?" I asked him.

"You got fucking jokes. I'm gonna fuck that bitch up when I see her," he said.

"Who? What happened anyway?" I asked.

"Leslie's bitch ass. That's what happened," he said.

"What did you do, cheat on her?"

"Hell nah. I wouldn't fuck that bitch with another nigga's dick. She's Sage's old bitch. He kicked her ass to the curb not too long ago. She's not feeling the whole earn your own money thing, so she came by the office the other day. I told her that Sage was gone, and he got married. She got pissed, and I had to throw her ass out. She called the police and told them that I beat her ass. I didn't though, not yet anyway."

"If you didn't, then why did she lie on you like that?" I asked.

"She couldn't get at Sage, so she got to me in order to get to him," he said.

"Does he know what's going on?"

"Nah, it's handled. The dumb bitch didn't know we got cameras in the fucking office. She told the cops that I beat her ass then threw her out. I had my secretary give the tapes to Montay, and he sent them up by my lawyer. I'm good. I just need somebody to fuck her ass up for real. She had somebody give her a black eye and all that basic shit, but I need her in the hospital for a few days. I told Sage she was gonna be a problem. He ain't believe me, though," Markos said.

"I'll do it," I told him.

"Nope, not happening. I know some hood chicks that don't have shit to lose. They'll do the shit if I pay a couple bills for them," Markos said.

"After everything that you've done for me, I owe you," I told him.

"Oh yeah, you owe me, huh. What you cooking?" he asked.

"Lasagna."

"Shit, you 'bout to get my ass fat. I gotta get back in the gym fucking with you," he said.

"You asked me to cook every Sunday, so that's what I'm doing. Let me know if you want to be a vegan or something, so I can change up the meals," I told him.

"Picture that shit. Stop by the store. I gotta get a bottle. You off today and tomorrow, so we gonna get lit tonight. You down for some strip poker?" Markos asked.

"Picture that shit," I told him.

This was what we did all the time now. We just hung out. Not really planning anything or even having any expectations regarding each other. We were just cool as shit.

We pulled up in the store parking lot, and he hopped out like he saw somebody he had a problem with, so I hopped out behind him.

"You mean to tell me they couldn't keep your ignorant ass locked up for the week at least?" some female said.

"You better be glad you a fucking female because I would kick your ass. You fucked up, coming for me. I'm not Sage. I don't give a fuck about you," Markos told her.

The chick laughed at him, but she looked nervous in the eyes. She looked at me then back to him a few times.

"Is this another cousin that you brought up here to beat me up for giving you a time out?" she said.

"No, don't worry about who she is," he said.

"Ohh, she must be important," she said. Then she looked at me. "I don't know who you are to him, but just know he's a Young. They don't know what love is. If you're looking for love, just leave his ass in this store. They are all male whores," she told me.

"You're just a transparent ass, gold digging, lazy ass chick," Markos said.

"And your dicks gonna fall off one day. Now that we have that out of the way, I'll leave you here with your little flavor of the month," she said.

Markos stepped up to me, pulled me into his arms, and tongued me down. When I say he kissed me, this nigga KISSED me. He had one of his hands palming my ass and all. When the kissing stopped, old girl was standing there with her mouth open.

"Baby, tell this bitch what it feels like to really kiss a Young.

We all know all Sage did was give her a kiss on the cheek or some shit, but she 'round here speaking on us and shit," Markos said.

She rolled her eyes and kissed her teeth. Markos walked away like it was nothing, and I walked behind him.

"You love making people think that we're a couple when we not, "I told him.

"You want anything out of here?" he asked me, ignoring what I said.

"No," I answered.

I knew he wasn't going to address what I said because that is just how Markos was. It was irritating as fuck, but I was used to it now.

We came out of the store to see my new truck decorated with FUCK THE YOUNGS in black spray paint. Now, mind you, my truck was pearl white. I looked up to see Markos staring at me.

"We'll see that bitch again. If you don't fuck her up when we do, me and you gonna fight. Now take me to your house. I'm tired and hungry," he said.

I could tell he was upset, so I didn't say anything. I pulled off wanting to see that bitch again.

Chapter Twenty-Two

22 – SAGE

I knew Nailah was pissed at me, but I really didn't mean for everything to come out like it did. I knew I had hurt her, but I honestly didn't mean to. She just didn't understand that right now we didn't need to be together like that. It would only further complicate everything.

She had a nigga in straight bitch mode trying to get at her. I had Leslie acting like she was in love with more than my money. I was helping her get right on paper, and my pops and hers were acting crazy and holding out info. That's why I had to put a stop to everything before it got started.

I had been out of town for a few days helping another client. We had been avoiding each other in the same house. I figured that she would be able to relax while I was gone. If I had known that all of this was going to happen, I would have told her no.

I pulled up to the house and wondered where her car was. It was too early for her to have been gone. Nailah was not a morning person, period. It wasn't even eleven in the morning, and her car was gone. I left my bags in the trunk because I knew that something was off. I opened the door, and I just knew off top that she had fucking moved out.

I headed straight for her room. Just like I thought, it was

empty. She didn't even leave anything to come back for. I walked back to the kitchen and tossed my keys on the table. That's when I saw my house and car keys that she was using. I tried to call her, but I kept going to voicemail. That only meant one thing; her ass had blocked me. So, I did the next best thing. I called Montay.

"Guess your ass just got home, huh?" he said when he answered.

"What the fuck is going on? I left to go to Chicago for three days, and my house empty and my number blocked. Where is she?" I asked him.

I knew he knew where she was. The questions was, would he tell me? We were all protective of her, even if that meant protecting her from each other. I knew I had hurt her, but we still had to be around each other. She didn't know, but I stayed on the outside of her door that morning. I heard her crying. It took everything in me to walk away from her like that. Truth be told, my feelings for her were way more than I was willing to admit or wanted to deal with right now. I just didn't expect for her to leave like she did.

"Nigga, she won't tell me what happened when y'all went away, but Stevie Wonder can see that something went down. She doesn't want to deal with your ass no more. She even asked me to have a sit down with you about the money situation. She wants me to fill her in on the progress. I even make the calls on how you invest or switch shit up. When she says she don't want you in her space, that's what the fuck she means. What did you do?" he asked.

"This is some bullshit," I said before ending the call.

Nailah never said anything about looking for a new place. Shit, after that night, she barely said anything to me at all. I should have known something, though. I thought I had some more time before she left me. Now I had no way of seeing her or even talking to her. I guess I didn't think this shit through.

Now, I had to figure out how to smooth this out with her. I

didn't need her avoiding me for the rest of our lives. The shit would be damn near impossible. Our families are too connected to be avoiding each other. I couldn't sit there and let her consume my mind like this I needed to get some sleep. If this shit got straight, it would do it on its own.

∞∞∞∞∞∞

After sleeping off and on all day, I needed to get out of the house. I decided to go catch a movie. I didn't feel like doing a club or a bar so the movies would have to do. It's been a minute since I've been to the movies, so I was going to choose something to see when I got there. I had my phone on do not disturb because I just was not feeling much of anything lately. I only came out because I felt like a sucker because of how I was feeling about a woman who wasn't even thinking about being mine. I was too fucking sexy to deal with this type of shit.

"What kind of popcorn do you want, beautiful?" I heard the nigga behind me say.

"Extra butter. I need my own small bag because I don't know where your hands been," she said with a giggle.

I put my head down because I wanted to slap the shit out of her right now. I listened to her fucking laugh and play like shit was all good with this lame ass nigga. I turned around because my head started hurting from not letting her know just who the fuck Sage Young really was.

"So, this is the shit you do after you move out of my house without a word?" I asked.

"Sage..." she said.

"Nah, answer the question," I said.

She started fidgeting like she was nervous.

"I think y'all need to talk about this another time. We're on a date, homie," the nigga said.

"I'm waiting for an answer. Then you out here with this

clown who clearly don't know the danger he's in just by being out here with you. So, this what we do? We protecting niggas now instead of being protected? You can't talk, or are you just acting like I'm calling and you blocking out what I say?" I asked her.

"Don't do this, Sage," she pleaded.

"Don't what, Nailah?" I asked. She chose not to answer, so that was my cue to show my entire ass. "Don't tell him that not too long ago you were screaming and pleading for me to cum in your pussy. Tight as your shit was, I never thought of you as one of these move around bitches. Look at ya trying to find another dick to fill you up like mine did. Is that what you want me to tell him? Huh? I can't hear you."

"Do you have to act like this?" she asked.

"You fucking right I gotta act like this. You got a nigga out here ready to kill you because you left his ass. You made me fall in love with you, just for me to come home to an empty house. Don't stand there and act like you didn't feel everything I felt that night. You had tears rolling down your face because we fucking fit together. The way your pussy massaged my dick was fucking epic, but you left my ass high and dry. I hope your stroke game is on point, nigga. That's if you get that far. Call me if you need a few pointers. I know this body like the back of my hand. Just like I know that thong is soaking wet right now. She probably can go to the bathroom and wring that motherfucker out like a wash rag. I hope Lox's crazy ass don't catch up with you while you out here," I said.

"Stop fucking acting like you care. You asked for this shit. You said it was only one night, right? So why you standing here acting like a fucking asshole because I'm doing what you told me to do. You wanted it, so you got it, now boss the fuck up and roll with it. Don't worry about Lox looking for me, I got this. After all, I'm a boss bitch in this motherfucker. Don't act like you didn't ask for this shit. You asked for it, now you got it. As for my thong, you'll never get that experience again, so let's hope you don't get amnesia or something because all you'll have is memories," she told me.

I watched her and that lame motherfucker walk away from me. I wanted to say more, but what she said was the truth. This was something that I asked for. I never thought that she would just pick up and go on with life just like that. I almost let her get to the door of the theater she was going into before I stopped her.

"Nailah, no matter how much you think about me when you're with him, he will never be me, Doll Baby," I told her.

I didn't want to see a movie anymore, so I left. While I was walking out the door, I saw a lady and her kid, so I gave her the movie tickets I had just bought. I needed to get home to a drink as soon as possible. Nailah Kahn was gonna be the death of me, but I couldn't stay away from her.

We were in for a bumpy ride. I hoped Lame Larry was ready for the ride he was going on. I'd be surprised if he lasted a week with Nailah. I didn't have shit to worry about.

Chapter Twenty-Three

23 - MARKOS

I had to have the dumbest cousin on the fucking planet right now. He'd been walking around here looking like a lost puppy behind Doll Baby. He still didn't tell me what went down when they were on vacation, but I had an idea of what it was. Montay was with us now discussing some financial moves that she needed to make soon. We could tell that Sage's mind was not focused on the shit we were discussing right now. He couldn't answer a damn question if I gave his ass the answer. I needed him to either get this shit off his chest and move on or go tell Nailah how he really felt.

"Do we need to put somebody else on Nailah's account? You looking pitiful as fuck right now," I told him.

I was only telling him the truth. He needed to get it together and quick. None of the other accounts were causing him to act like this, so it had to be her. There was no other conclusion to be made.

"Why you keep bringing her up?" Sage asked me.

"Because we not stupid. You acting stupid, and she's acting like a straight bitch. What happened on vacation? Spill it, nigga, we brothers here. What's up?" Montay asked.

Sage stood up and walked to his window. He was looking out the window like someone was out there looking back at his ass.

"We made love," he said.

Montay and I looked at each other like we couldn't understand what he was saying.

"Y'all fucked?" Montay asked.

"No, we didn't fuck or just have sex. That shit had me ready to either wife her or knock her ass up. I don't know if it was the island liquor or just the stress of everything going on, but that shit was like nothing I've ever experienced before. The shit was epic," he told us.

"So, why y'all not together?" I asked.

"It's not the time for all of that. She got her shit to handle. I've still got Leslie to handle. All the outside shit will tear us apart. I don't need that. I don't want her to end up hating me," Sage said.

"Too late. She most likely doesn't hate you right now, but she's close as hell to it. Now that she's with old dude, she don't want me to say your name at all. I have to call you 'my cousin.' The shit is pretty funny to me," Montay said and laughed.

I could see it on Sage's face that he wanted to choke the shit out of Nailah.

"So, you shut it down before it got started?" I asked him.

"Yeah," he answered.

"Okay, so look. Baltimore is gonna kick Leslie's ass when she sees her. Just wanted to give you a heads up and shit. We still haven't seen her since she did that shit to Baltimore's truck. I know she only did the shit because she couldn't get her hands on you, but the shit is fucked up," I told him.

I always knew that Leslie was a weak bitch. I told Sage over and over again that she wasn't the one for him. He thought I was just saying that because she was a lazy, gold digging ass hoe. It was more than that. The bitch wasn't loyal and didn't know shit about doing something for anybody but herself. In my book, she was the worst kind of chick out there. She didn't think she did shit wrong when her being involved was wrong as hell. The money was nothing because we had plenty of that shit.

She's the chick you hold down, and as soon as you get picked up for driving with a suspended license, she already at the bank telling the bank teller that she's your wife and she needs to get in your account. That type of disloyalty made me want to snap her neck every time I saw her. That's why I didn't respect her ass. I told her exactly how I felt when I saw her with no fucking filter. Fuck her feelings.

"You want me to handle her?" Sage asked.

"No. Let her keep fucking with me and B. I can use this to make B realize that she cares about a nigga. You don't need any more bullshit in your world right now. I think she's gonna eventually try to get your ass, but she don't know shit. We're clean, but the rest of the family is dirty as a pig's ass in slop. Let her keep thinking she winning," I told him.

"Who the fuck you think you are? Why you calling old girl B? She not Beyoncé, and you damn sure ain't Hov," Montay said.

"Shorty my Beyoncé," I sang like I was Dirk the rapper.

"What y'all got going on today?" Sage asked us.

"I'm going to make B fall for a nigga some more. I almost got her where I want her. You should have seen her face when she thought Leslie was one of my crazy exes." I laughed.

"I gotta go to the prison to check on Ruff. He says he wanna put me on some shit that might help him out," Montay said.

I shook my head because Montay always went hard for Ruff's hardheaded ass. Ruff was this lil nigga from around the way. The nigga was a beast on the football field. His mom was the typical black mother working her ass off too damn hard to see that her child was gonna be lost to the streets. It wasn't shit that she was doing wrong, that's just how shit went sometimes.

Montay tried to help Ruff get his shit together, but it was too late. Montay had been telling him to leave these knuckleheads alone that Ruff had been hanging with. Ruff never listened. One night, they were hanging out together when shit went bad. Ruff didn't know that his so-called friends had just robbed a fucking corner store. I didn't know why or how they ended up being pulled over, but when they did, the cops found shit from the robbery in the car, and they all got arrested.

I knew Montay was still communicating with Ruff, and that's what they both needed. Montay didn't have shit to take care of, not even a dog. Ruff made everybody know that his ass had a heart. I still say he should just fuck Ruff's mama and give that lil nigga a brother or a sister. Montay wasn't trying to hear that, though with his dry dick having ass.

"You still helping that nigga?" Sage said.

"The nigga needs somebody. He ain't got nobody but his mom, and she works like a fucking Jamaican. It's all good. He's a good kid, he just needs some guidance," Montay said.

"He needs a boot up his ass. It's like what you doing, though. You gonna got some good karma behind it," Sage said.

"Keep that bitch named karma away from me. I've done some fucked up shit in my day. I don't need her showing up when I might have found a bitch I don't wanna choke," I told them.

Hearing about karma had my ass nervous. I didn't need some fucked up shit in my atmosphere. I wasn't scared of nobody, but that bitch karma was one bitch that I was running from. That's why I was hoping Baltimore would be the one that I could settle down with and maybe have a future with a couple years from now. My phone ringing had those two niggas looking at me like I was crazy.

"Let me find out she got you actually putting your phone in your pocket now. You never bring your phone with you. It's always in your fucking car. What's really good?" Montay asked me.

I ignored him and answered my call.

"Sup," I answered.

"Why is there a fucking Tesla in front of my house?" Baltimore yelled in my ear.

"You got some nigga coming to see you, I guess. Do you see anybody out there?" I asked her, trying not to laugh.

"You are the only person I know with money that long. I thought you were just gonna get my truck fixed. What happened? There's no way I can pay you back. Whose name is on the title?" she asked.

"Why you need to know whose name is on it?"

I was almost scared of her answer. Baltimore had an imagination that would have you questioning shit you knew was the truth.

"If your name is on it, that means one day I could wake up, and it's not where I parked it. It also says that you not really rocking with me like that. You just don't want me to be seen out here in a bucket because people see us together. I'm not sexing you up or anything. As far as I know, we're just friends. You could find the love of your life and forget all about me," she said.

I looked at the phone to see if I was talking to the right person because Baltimore didn't sound like herself. Sure enough, it was her number on the phone.

"Drive the car or don't drive the car. I really don't fucking care. What happened to saying thank you when people try to do nice shit for you? I'll be there in a little bit, man. You better be there when I get there," I told her before banging in her fucking face.

These two fools were laughing at my ass like I was a comedian or something. I sat there fucking pissed at the fact that she was wilding out on my ass. She was about to see another side of me as soon as I got to where she was.

Chapter Twenty-Four

24 – NAILAH

"Have you talked to that guy yet?" Ralph asked me.

I rolled my eyes because I was getting annoyed at answering the same question over and over again. Since the night at the theater, he had been asking about my connection to Sage. I didn't tell him anything because it really isn't his business to know, and I didn't want to talk about it. He was constantly bothering me about Sage.

"No," I simply said.

"If you ask me, you need to talk to him. If we're gonna be together, then he needs to know his boundaries. How did he know you were there anyway?" he asked.

"It's a fucking movie theater. That is a public place, and he is free to move around just like us. Sage and I have nothing to discuss. I told you already that I'm not getting in a relationship with you or anyone else. I'm not in the right mind space to be anybody's girlfriend. You and I are just friends. If you're looking for more than that, I can't help you," I told him.

He could act like he was hurt all he wanted. I had been telling him this from the first conversation we had. It was not my fault he thought he could change my mind.

"Do you even have a heart?" Ralph asked me.

"I'm just gonna leave now before you ask me another stupid ass question. Yes, I have a heart. How do you think I'm alive and breathing?" I asked him.

"You know what I mean, Nailah, don't be sarcastic," he said.

"No, to be honest, I don't have a heart. The last mother-fucker I gave my body to took it from me. I didn't give it to him, but he didn't steal it either. If you want something deep and mesmerizing, I'm not the one for all that. I just want a companion to have fun with who won't drag me down into a pit of emotional bullshit," I told him.

"Is that Sage guy the one who took your heart?" Ralph asked.

"Goodbye Ralph," I told him.

I walked away from the table, not even caring if he called me or not. Ralph was trying to make me his woman, and that is the one thing I will never be. He may think that I'm just playing hard to get or something like that, but I'm really not. My heart and soul are off limits, even to me.

I was walking around looking all put together without a hair out of place or a nail not painted. Inside, I was in shambles, all because of Sage. I hated that he had a hold on me like he did. I was thinking of this man all the time. I had dreams of him when I went to sleep. I was a pitiful case right now, and no one would ever know.

I got to my car, and low and behold, the fucking boogie man was sitting on my hood. I did pause a step or two, but only for a second. I got in the car as if he wasn't there. I went to start it, but nothing happened. When I looked, up he was standing there with a smirk on his face.

"What the fuck did you do to my car, Lox?" I asked him as I got out.

"I'm ready to come back home," Lox said seriously.

"Why are you telling me? The house we lived in has been sold. You can call home wherever you've been sleeping at night," I told him.

I took my phone out and texted the security detail that Sage had on me. I had put the duck on them when I left the house this morning. Right now, I was regretting that decision. I didn't like the look in Lox's eyes. It was like he was a new person or something.

"How are you gonna let those Youngs take over what your father built? I know you have one of those niggas in my spot. I never thought that you would be so fucking gullible to believe what some bitch tells you. DeJa knew all about you. She was just pissed that I chose you over her. Spiteful ass bitches will do anything to get some attention," Lox said.

"What about the bitch that you said you were with when you called her that day? I know she wasn't the only one. DeJa, on the other hand, was blind to that fact. You really had her believing that she was the only other woman. We have nothing to talk about, Lox. You need to let me go and accept your consequences. You fucked up, plain and simple," I told him.

"You didn't have to fire me, though. Now you got me out here looking crazy as hell," He said.

"I don't have you looking no kind of way. You did all this. You couldn't keep your dick in your pants, but everything you're dealing with is everybody else's fault. How fucked up does that sound?" I said.

This nigga had lost his mind since we broke up. He still hadn't admitted his wrongs, and it looked like he never will. A black truck came speeding toward me. I knew it was the security detail, and I guess Lox did too.

"Tell your man and his cousins that it's about to get hot," Lox said before walking off.

The security guys got out of the car looking pissed that I had put the duck on them. It wasn't their fault. I used to duck my security all the time when I was a teenager. I was probably more experienced at this shit then they were.

"Are you okay? I'm gonna have to call the boss to let him know what happened," one of the guys said.

"Can you pop my hood to find out why my car won't start?" I asked, ignoring everything he had just said.

The other guy lifted the hood, and Lox had cut every wire in sight. I was like he got under there and didn't know what the hell he was doing.

"Where did your lunch date go?" one of them asked.

"We had a disagreement," I answered.

I saw a silver Bentley pull up. I knew it was Sage, but I didn't want to deal with him. I didn't know what he was pulling up for. I was sure his guys told him that I was okay. There was no need for him to drive up. The windows were tinted, but I knew who it was. The car was just sitting on the opposite side of the street. No one got out of the car or anything. It was just sitting there with windows tinted so dark that I couldn't see who was behind the wheel.

"I called the tow truck, but we'll take you back home or to run your errands," one of the security guys said.

I hopped in the back of the truck. As I was getting in, I saw the Bentley finally pull off. I shook my head because he did all of that for what? I was irritated with all men right now. Ralph and his dumb questions, Lox and his bullshit, now Sage riding around acting like Batman and shit. Were there any normal men in the world anymore.

∞∞∞∞∞

I was sitting alone in my living room with music playing in the background. I really needed to get out more. I didn't have one person that I could call a true friend. In fact, I was such a sad case that the only friends I had were Montay and Markos. I had to laugh at that fact.

I didn't want to be in the house alone again, so I got up to get dressed. I was going out somewhere if I had to go out alone.

When I was done taking my shower and putting my clothes on, I headed out the door.

"Where you going?" he said as I reached for the door.

"Do you always break into houses and sit in the corner?" I asked him.

"Answer the question Do you have another project with the lame nigga outreach program?"

"Why are you even here, Sage?" I asked.

"I just came to check on you," he said.

"Usually when people want to check on a person, they knock on the door or call them on the phone. They don't break in houses," I told him.

"Ain't shit about me usual or regular. When were you gonna tell me that Lox approached you today?" he asked.

"I wasn't. I'm not your concern anymore. In all reality, I never was. I just went with the flow of everything, but you stopped all that," I told him.

"You will always be my concern. I don't give a fuck about what you say. I know you don't think that lame nigga gonna do shit to anybody if they come at you," Sage said.

"Sage, get out. I'm trying to go out and enjoy my evening. You're fucking up my vibe," I told him.

He looked at me and smirked. Then he started looking me up and down, licking his lips and shit. I knew you had to actually have sex to get pregnant, but the way he was looking at me was something terrible. It was like that night came rushing back to me out of nowhere. My body was going crazy. I hadn't been this close to Sage since that night. I cussed my body out because I knew that after he left, I would have to take another shower.

He stepped closer to me.

"I miss you, Doll Baby," he whispered to me.

I didn't respond because in my head we were already fucking. He had me bent over the couch squeezing my ass as he hit it from the back. My hair was wrapped up in his hand as if I was running from MY dick. I could feel him inside me, causing me to moan out loud.

I stepped away from him because I was getting too wrapped up in my emotions. I didn't need to do this with him ever again. This was not what we both needed. There was just a strong lust between us.

I moved to the other side of the room. Sage was still standing in the same spot. I guess he was just as lost as I was because he was looking through me and gripping his dick. He was hard as a motherfucker. Sage didn't take his eyes off me, and I didn't take mine off him. I don't know when it happened, but the next thing I knew, Sage Young was standing in my hallway beating his dick and looking dead at me.

I wanted to move, maybe even cuss his ass out, but none of that happened. I stood there and watched this man ejaculate on my hardwood floors. The bad thing is, I almost had an orgasm of my own just by looking at him. When he was finished, he walked over to me with his dick still out. I was still standing there like a fucking idiot. He kissed me, not just a regular kiss, either. He kissed me deeply, like down to the depths of my soul kiss. He took his hand and caressed my treasure under my dress and through my soaked panties.

"I'm fucking starving for you. You ruined me, Nailah," he said.

I was trying to get my body to follow my mind and get away from him. Instead, my legs stayed open. I felt him rip my thong off, and he was inside me just like that. It shouldn't feel this good for him to be inside me like this. He stroked my insides repeatedly.

"Sage, I love you. I love you," I screamed out.

"I will always love you. Don't forget that shit, ever," he said directly in my ear.

All of a sudden there was a phone ringing. I jumped up off the couch, only to be disappointed that this was another dream about Sage and I. I was soaking wet with sweat. I must have fallen asleep on the couch while looking at TV. The clock said three in the morning. Who the fuck was calling me at three in the morning? I looked at the phone and saw that Lox had called me ten times. Just like his ass to fuck up a banging ass wet dream.

25 – BALTIMORE

I was sitting my ass right in the living room waiting on Billy Bad Ass to walk through my door. He had me fucked up if he thought he was gonna buy me. I didn't appreciate how he was moving now. In the beginning, everything was cool. We both understood that we were just friends and that's it. Now he was acting like a father or a boyfriend.

I heard the key go in the door, and I sat up because we were gonna hash this shit out today. If he had to leave here with his groceries, car, and whatever else he bought me, then it would get done.

"Now what was that shit you were saying on the phone?" he asked when he walked in.

"You need to make some shit clear to me. We both are obviously looking at this two different ways," I told him.

"Your truck got fucked up because of me. I went out and got you something hotter to ride in. There ain't a damn thing confusing about that," he said.

"I got a date tonight," I said, just to see what he was gonna say.

"Nah, no you don't," he replied.

"Yes, I do," I said.

"Don't get fucked up, B. You not going on no fucking date," he fussed.

"Why not? I'm single as hell, and I'm tired of buying batteries," I said with a smile.

"Keep thinking this shit is a game," he said.

"What is this exactly? What are we doing, Markos? You claim we not together, but you always get pissed when I mention another man or a date. You confusing me right now. I'm not understanding what's going on between us. I'm liking you a little too much for us to be just friends. I can admit that," I told him.

"You my girl," he said.

"Your girl? What the fuck does that mean?" I asked.

"We together, a couple, like Jay and Bey. I look way better than Jay, but you know what I mean. You my girl. I know I should have been told you what it was with us. Real shit, I like you, and I'm not letting you go. Why you think I make it a point to talk to you every day? I do that shit because I'm digging you. I'm thinking about you all fucking day," he told me.

"Do I have a choice in this?" I asked him.

"Do you need a fucking choice?" he countered.

"Why couldn't you just talk to me about this? I shouldn't have to force you to tell me anything."

"I know. I'm just not the type of nigga who talks a lot of shit. I'd rather show you what shit is instead. I know you hate me spending money on you and shit, but that's the main way I know how to show chicks that I care. I'm not trying to buy you or no shit like that. I just want you to understand that you mean a lot to me," he told me.

"You need to take that Tesla back and go get me a Honda or a Dodge," I told him.

"No. I can't do that. You not gonna be my girl riding around in no shit like that. I'll get you a Beemer or a Mercedes if you don't want the Tesla. That's as low as I'm going with the cars. You have to let ya nigga spoil you. You deserve it, and so much more," he said.

I could tell by looking at him that he was serious about his words. He was always caring and considerate to me. I don't know how he did other folks, but he made me happy.

"You need to call that scrub that you had a date with to let him know not to call you no more. You not going out on a date unless it's with me," Markos fussed.

I laughed at him because he knew that I didn't have a date. I walked over to where he was sitting and straddled his lap facing him. He smiled up at me. It was nice to finally get to touch him how I wanted to. He kept looking at me and playing in my hair.

"Don't ever change your hair color. This red looks sexy on your ass. I don't care if you sixty or eighty years old, keep this color, man," he told me.

I leaned in to kiss his lips. Feeling his big strong arms around me made me tingle on the inside. We kept kissing as he caressed my ass. He was setting my body on fire. He kissed all over my neck then he took my shirt off. I was scared at first, but once he looked at me then back down with so much compassion and care, I relaxed.

"Where did you get this from?" he asked.

I closed my eyes as I felt him run his hand across the scar above my left breast. I had been years since I talked about what happened that night. I wanted to tell him so many times, but I never found the words to say it. A tear fell from my eyes.

He wiped it away before it could fall to my chin.

"My stepfather stabbed me one night when I chose to fight him off instead of letting him have his way. It had been going on for years, being that my mom worked the night shift. My brother, Brooklyn, came rushing in. He saw me on the ground bleeding from my chest, and he went off and beat my stepdad to death that night. I was taken to the hospital, and after surgery and weeks in a coma, I came to.

"I was happy at first to see my mother there with me because that meant that she was standing by my side. Then she opened her mouth. She told me that I had taken everyone away from her. My stepdad was dead, and my brother got locked up for fifteen years. She told me I was dead to her and she never wanted to see me again. That was the last I heard from her. I send my brother money on his books when I can. I don't have enough nerve to go see him yet. It's been six years. Once I was cleared, I moved up here, and this is where I've been ever since," I told him.

"Why haven't you gone to see your brother?" he asked.

"If I didn't fight my stepfather, he would be free. I would still have my family, and my mother wouldn't hate me," I told him.

"Whenever you ready, we gonna go together. Give me his info so I can make sure bro-in-law is straight. You need to think about going to see him. I know you may think that all of this is your fault, but he did what a brother is supposed to do. He was protecting you. Don't keep your back turned on him. He may need you the same way you need him. Family is important, Baltimore. Even though your mom is out there acting like she don't have any kids, you should never treat your brother like that," he told me.

I had gone back and forth for years about how I needed to go see Brooklyn. I just never had the confidence to do it. I thought about my brother all the time. I loved him. I just had to deal with the fact that his love for me had landed him in jail. I still wondered about my mother, even though she'd written me off for dead. I will always love her. I didn't understand her actions, but I loved her just the same.

I wanted Markos to come over to talk about us, and here I am balling like Weeping Wanda in his arms. I tried to get up, but he held me tighter. I eventually stopped trying to get away from him.

"Don't you ever keep some shit like this in. If you hurting, you supposed to let me know so I can take the pain away from you. As your man, I'm supposed to carry the weight. You don't need to worry about shit, I don't care how big or small it is. If I find out you stressing, I'm gonna fuck you up. I'm not gonna ask questions either. We're gonna have to communicate if we gonna rule the world," he told me.

I had to laugh at him because he can be so crazy sometimes. I was used to him by now. He was my man now, so I guess you could say that I was just as crazy as he was.

Chapter Twenty-Six

26 - MONTAY

I hated coming to this fucking place. Unfortunately, I couldn't put this shit off on anybody else right now. Ruff had better be glad I took his hard-headed ass under my wing. I should have gotten to him earlier, but hopefully, this shit wouldn't be too hard to get him out of.

"Hey, Montay. What's good, man? You up here to see young buck?" Officer Jones asked.

Me and Jones grew up in the same hood. Other than the nigga getting a job up here, he was a cool motherfucker. He didn't hang out much because it was impossible for him not to run into the same motherfuckers he was watching in there day in and day out. I understood his point, so it was what it was. I knew that if I needed anything, he would be there for me. Which is why I had him looking out for Ruff while he was in there.

"He doing alright in here?" I asked.

"That lil nigga is fine. He had some niggas testing him, but he handled that shit. I wasn't too far away watching it all go down. He can handle himself, you don't have to worry," Jones told me.

"Good looking out. How's the family? How's ya fine ass mama?" I asked laughing.

"You think this badge gonna save you? I told your ass stop talking 'bout my damn mama," he said.

I always fucked with him about his mama. I don't know what she was doing, but whatever it was had her giving these young girls out here a run for their money. If I was into older chicks, she would be at the top of my list. I know I caught her ass looking at me a couple times when I saw her or on the street.

"Man, fuck you. I'm 'bout to be your step-daddy. Did you clean your room before you came to work today?" I asked him and laughed.

He shook his head at me as he laughed too. The people around us were looking at us like we were crazy, but we just went back like four flats on a Cadillac. We kept talking about bullshit as I followed him into the visiting room. It was packed as usual with all the mules and freaky ass girlfriends or wives wearing short ass skirts with tight ass shirts. Niggas never got enough of putting their women in danger. You not a real man if you can't keep your woman out of harm's way, even if that meant that he had to die in the process. I looked around and waited for Ruff to bring his ass out, and that's when I saw her. It had been years, but I knew it was her.

She had to be visiting. I knew damn well she wasn't an inmate. If she was an inmate, what the fuck did she do to get in there? Did anybody know where she was? Damn, she was still fucking beautiful. That long, black silky hair wasn't down to her ass like the last time I saw her, but it was past her shoulders. Her skin was flawless as fuck. I didn't want to stare too hard, but I needed to see if it was really her.

Nobody knew where the fuck she was. They couldn't the way Nailah cried to Sage about her being gone. The Niggas she was talking to at her table didn't look like any ordinary niggas. They were fucking Feds, I could tell that shit from a mile away. *What the hell is really going on?*

"Montay!" Ruff called out all loud and shit.

His loud ass made everybody look up, including her. She saw me looking at her, and the color from her face went away. She jumped up, staring at me just like I was staring at her. Then she turned and rushed out of the room. The police were calling out a name that didn't belong to her. She didn't look back or break her stride. I watched her disappear around the corner before heading straight to Officer Jones.

"Since when do y'all house female prisoners?" I asked him.

"Only the important ones or the ones they trying to hide why? What's up?" he asked.

"The chick that just left out of here, do you know why she's in here?" I asked.

"You talking about mystery meat. We call her that because she in here under a name that's not hers and only federal agents come to see her. Either she's in some deep shit, or she knows some deep shit," he said.

I came in there to help Ruff out, and the answer to a long lost family question fell into my lap. This shit was making my neck hot. I wrote down Sage's phone number on a piece of paper and handed it to Jones.

"Get this number to her and tell her to call it as soon as possible. If you gotta let her use your phone, do it. It's important as a motherfucker that this call gets made. What name is she in here under?" I asked him.

"Susan Smith," he said.

"The white chick that killed her kids?" I asked.

"Yup, that's the same thing I said," Jones told me.

"I thought you came to see me, Montay?" Ruff said with his smart ass mouth.

"Nigga, shut your dumb ass up. If you had left those knuckleheads alone, you wouldn't be here in the first fucking place," I told him to shut his ass up.

"Come on, man, I told you it was my bad on that bullshit," Ruff said.

I shook my head at him. I gave Jones the head nod, and he walked away. I knew that Jones would make sure the message got to where it was supposed to go. I just hoped she used the number like I needed her to.

I sat down at the table and halfway listened to Ruff tell me how his so called boys told the police that he was the one behind everything. I listened to him talk and wondered if this was going wake his ass up. He needed to learn that just because they call you a friend, it doesn't mean they *are your friend.*

"Just keep your head down, stay out of bullshit. I'll do what I can do to get you out of here. Once I get you out, you need to get your shit together, go to school, or get a trade or something. I'll help you out, just stay away from those knuckleheads," I told him.

After leaving the visiting area, I immediately called Sage to have him and Markos meet me at Pop's house. I had to tell them about what I just saw.

∞∞∞∞∞∞

I pulled up, and they were all there waiting for me. I rushed in the house, which was only for dramatic effect, but it was funny as hell to see their faces. I knew they were in the middle of a conversation, but I didn't care.

"Did you ever ask Kahn what happened to his wife? I'm saying, did he even look for her?" I asked Pops.

"No. We argued about it then I just stopped talking to him. The shit just didn't feel right to me. What him and Nadia had was on the level of me and my wife. I would never have her somewhere missing and not look for her. I wanted to kill his ass my damn self," Pops fussed.

"Why you asking about Nailah's mom?" Sage asked.

"I saw her today at the prison," I answered.

"WHAT!" they all yelled together.

"No bullshit. I saw her with my own eyes. She's been there from what I can tell. She was meeting with some federal agents. She's there under a false name. They gave her ass the name Susan Smith. She's the chick who killed her kids and blamed a black guy for it. That's the name they gave her," I told them.

"Did you talk to her?" Sage asked.

"No, I was going to talk to her, but Ruff called my name before I could get to her. She left, but I..." I tried to explain, but Sage's phone rang.

I gave Sage a head nod, letting him know to answer the phone.

"Hello," Sage answered.

"Put it on speaker," I said.

"I was given this number by one of the guards here. I don't know who I'm supposed to be talking to or why," she said.

"Nadia! What the hell are you doing in prison? Does Kahn know where you are? How long have you been there?" Pops asked.

"Maurice, is that you? You can't tell anyone where I am. Kahn doesn't know, and it's best that way. I'm here to keep everyone else out of here," she said.

"What the fuck does that mean? Everyone has been worried sick about you, and this is where you've been? I need some fucking answers, and I'm gonna get them," Pops said.

"Stay away from this and away from me. I'm begging you. This way is better for everybody, believe me," she pleaded.

"You belong out here, Nadia. This is bullshit. If Kahn is behind this, I'm going to kick his ass," Pops roared.

"Maurice, it's not worth it. Everything is much better this way. Believe me, please. I did this so EVERYONE could stay free. Don't worry about me. Just keep my baby girl safe. I sacrificed myself for all of you. Don't waste the time that you have," she said.

"Nadia, what the fuck is going on? Do you fucking hear me? I asked you a fucking question," Pops yelled.

"She hung up. Why you so worked up, Pops? If anything, Kahn should be worked up, not you. What's missing?" Sage asked.

"What the fuck you mean why am I so worked up? Your mother lost her best friend. Her and Nadia had been friends since elementary school. Nadia walking away like she did started your mother's broken heart. On top of that, I lost my best friend because of the same thing. This family has been broken for a long time, and this situation was the first crack that started it all. Now to hear that she's in prison is just bringing up all of those emotions again. Montay, call Kahn's number and put that motherfucker on speaker," Pops said.

I pulled out my phone and dialed Kahn's number.

"Hello," Kahn answered.

"I need you and Nailah in my living room like fifteen minutes ago. I'm not fucking playing either, nigga. Get your ass up and get over here. Both of y'all," Pops said.

"What's going on? Is everybody okay?" Kahn asked.

"Evidently shit ain't okay if I'm calling you. This isn't anything that needs to be discussed on the phone. See you when you both get here," Pops said.

He nodded his head, so I ended the call. Sage started to shift in his seat. I knew he was feeling some type of way about being in front of Nailah again, but I knew Pops wasn't gonna let him leave either.

"Son, I know you over there squirming and shit because you fucked up. I don't know for sure what went down with you two, but I know you are a fucking Young before anything. You and Nailah are going to have a lot more arguments before it's all said and done. I need you to be ten fingers up with this. She's gonna need you now more than ever. You know she's stubborn as fuck, so get ready. I'm glad you finally left Lolita alone too," Pops said.

We all started laughing because he just knew he was still young out here.

"It's ten toes down, Unc. If it was ten fingers up, that would mean he's waving at her with both hands." Marios laughed.

"Why y'all gotta be so difficult these days? Ten toes down don't make sense either. Sage, listen to me, son. Whatever y'all mad about, put it to the side. She needs you just like you need to protect her. Don't let anything else get in the way. If you had waited to fuck her until all of this was over, you wouldn't be looking like that," Pops said.

"Yo, you fucked Doll Baby?" Markos asked all dramatic like he didn't know already.

"I know you two niggas already knew. There ain't much you don't tell each other, so stop the bullshit, Markos," Pops said

Sage just shook his head.

"We not fucking. She asked me to make love to her, so I did. The shit was way too intense, so I told her we needed to fall back from all that other shit," Sage said.

Pops started laughing like Sage told a joke. I admit the shit sounded dumb to me, but it wasn't that damn funny.

"Just let us know who you want to be your best man. I'm telling you right now if I'm not the one, I'm gonna kick your ass," Pops said laughing.

"You think this is real funny, huh, old man?" Sage asked.

"Nigga, yeah I'm old, but my dick is still big. At least I'm not sitting over there looking stupid in the face," Pops said.

We all laughed because Sage knows that Pops doesn't have a lick of common sense. There was a knock at the door, and Markos went to answer it. A few seconds later, in walked Kahn and Nailah. Kahn looked irritated, and Nailah was looking at Sage.

"What the fuck is going on?" Kahn asked.

Pop stood up and put his hands in his pocket.

"Nadia didn't run off into the sunset. She's in prison under an alias. She says that she's there to help keep us out of jail. She doesn't want you to know, but we gotta find a way to bring her home," Pops said.

Kahn sat down, trying to digest what Pops had just said.

"That ain't it," Pops said.

"You just told me that Nadia is in prison. What else could be just as important as that?" Kahn asked.

"Calm your ass down. I just wanted to tell you to get your tux out the closet. Our kids are fucking, nigga. Get the wedding speech out. We about to be family," Pops said and laughed.

Nailah looked like she was gonna die, and Sage looked pissed. Nailah ran out, and Sage went behind her.

"You a damn trip, Unc," I told him.

"Yeah, alright. They talking, ain't they?" Pops said, still laughing.

"What are the charges they have Nadia under?" Kahn asked.

"I don't know, and I really don't care. I'm asking you right now, what do you want to do?" Pops asked.

"Let's go get my fucking wife," Kahn said.

Get LiT!

Download the LiT app today and enjoy exclusive content, free books, and more!

Join our mailing list to get a notification when Leo Sullivan
Presents has another release!
Text LEOSULLIVAN to 22828 to join!
To submit a manuscript for our review, email us at
submissions@leolsullivan.com